BEST GAY ROMANCE 2008

BEST GAY ROMANCE 2008

Edited by
Richard Labonté

CLEIS
PRESS

Cleis Press Inc., P.O. Box 14697, San Francisco, California 94114
Printed in the United States.
Cover design: Scott Idleman
Cover photograph: Celesta Danger
Text design: Frank Wiedemann
Cleis logo art: Juana Alicia
First Edition.
10 9 8 7 6 5 4 3 2 1

For Asa, best romance ever

Contents

INTRODUCTION

Romance. It's the emotional component of the erotic. Sucking and fucking are the easy parts. The hard part is falling in love. That's what this collection is all about—the many ways one man woos and wins another. Sometimes it lasts for one intense hour. Sometimes it waxes, and then wanes. Sometimes it lasts forever. However romance happens, however long love lasts—a heartbeat to a lifetime—it's a wondrous thing.

It happens in Jay Starre's "Fucked on Kilimanjaro" as two hot men climb the cold slopes of a mountain. It happens in J. M. Snyder's "Henry and Jim" when two old men reflect on years gone by. It happens in Max Pierce's "Viva Las Vegas" when a man in a tuxedo redeems a disastrous date. It happens in T. Hitman's "The Bike Path" when companions forever take a ride together. It happens in Shanna Germain's "Coming Home" when two boyhood buddies reconnect while hefting bales of hay.

It happens in Jack Fritscher's "The Rush of Love" when a muscle admirer plays all night with a muscle god. It happens in Natty Soltesz's "A Not-So-Straight Duet" when teen boys cross over a very queer line. It happens in Dale Chase's "The Empire Room" when hearts connect while mourning. It happens in Rob Rosen's "Gone Fishing" when a dream man is lost then found again. It happens in Kal Cobalt's "The Belt"—at the end of a belt.

Sometimes romance is a fairy tale: that's one magical part of Shaun Levin's "Boyfriends: A Triptych." Sometimes the memory of romance hurts: Simon Sheppard explores that pain in "Falling." Sometimes ghosts from the past have the power to shape a couple's future: Jameson Currier imagines just that in "The Country House." Sometimes love heals, truly heals: Victor J. Banis illuminates the possibility in "The Canals of Mars." Sometimes the flame of romance flickers: Jason Shults confronts that reality in "What the Eye Reveals." And sometimes the world conspires to snuff out the flame: Matthew Lowe writes heart-rendingly about two boys in love and their wistful fate.

Sex happens in our lives, and some of the sixteen stories in this collection are as sexually rough as they are romantically tender. Whether rowdy or mushy, though, these tales celebrate the coming together of souls as well as of bodies—the wonderful possibility of *happily ever after*.

Richard Labonté
Calabogie, Ontario/Bowen Island, British Columbia
September 2007

HENRY AND JIM

J. M. Snyder

His folded hands are pale and fragile in the early morning light, the faint veins beneath translucent skin like faded ink on forgotten love letters written long ago. His fingers lace through mine; his body curves along my back, still asleep despite the sun that spills between the shades. I lie awake for long minutes, clasped tight against him, unable or unwilling to move and bring the day crashing in. Only in sleep am I sure that he fully remembers me. When he wakes, the sun will burn that memory away and I'll have to watch him struggle to recall my name. After a moment or two he'll get it without my prompting but one day I know it will be gone, lost like the dozen other little things he no longer remembers, and no matter how long I stare into his weathered blue eyes, he won't be able to get it back.

Cradled in his arms, I squeeze his hands in my arthritic fists and pray this isn't that day.

After some time he stirs, his even breath breaking with a shuddery sigh that tells me he's up. There's a scary moment when he freezes against me, unsure of where he is or who I am. I hold my breath and wait for the moment it all falls into place. His thumb smoothes along my wrist, and an eternity passes before he kisses behind my ear, my name a whisper on his lips. "Henry."

I sigh, relieved. Today he still remembers, and that gives me the strength to get out of bed. "Morning, Jim." I stretch like an old cat, first one arm then the other, feeling the blush of energy as my blood stirs and familiar aches settle into place. Over my shoulder I see Jim watching, a half smile on his face that tells me he still likes what he sees. As I reach for my robe, I ask him, "How about some eggs this morning? That sound good?"

"You know how I like them," he says, voice still graveled from sleep. His reply wearies me—I don't know if he's forgotten how he prefers his eggs or if he simply trusts me to get them right. I want to believe in his trust, so I don't push it. After fifty years of living with Jim, of loving him, I choose my battles carefully, and this isn't one either of us would win.

Leaning across the bed, I plant a quick kiss on the corner of his mouth. "Be down in ten minutes," I murmur.

His gnarled fingers catch the knot in the belt of my robe and keep me close. My lower back groans in protest, but I brush the wisps of white hair from his forehead and smile through the discomfort as he tells me, "I have to shower."

"Jim," I sigh. When I close my eyes he's eighteen again, the fingers at my waist long and graceful and firm, his gaunt cheeks smooth and unwrinkled, his lips a wet smile below dark eyes and darker hair. It pains me to have to remind him, "We showered last night."

He runs a hand through his thinning hair, then laughs. "Ten minutes then," he says with a playful poke at my stomach. I catch his hand in mine and lean against it heavily to help myself up.

We met in the late spring, 1956, when I graduated from State. It seems so long ago now—it's hard to imagine we were ever anything but the old men we've become. My youngest sister Betty had a boy she wanted me to meet, someone I thought she was courting at the time, and she arranged an afternoon date. I thought she wanted my approval before she married the guy; that's the way things were done back in the day. But when I drove up to Jim's parents' house and saw those long legs unfold as he pushed himself up off the front steps of the porch, I thought I'd spend the rest of my life aching for him. I could just imagine the jealousy that would eat me alive, knowing my sister slept in those gangly arms every night; family gatherings would become unbearable as I watched the two of them kiss and canoodle together. By the time he reached my car, I decided to tell Betty she had to find someone else. That nice Italian kid on the corner perhaps, or the McKeever's son around the block. Anyone but this tall, gawkish man-boy with the thin face and unruly mop of dark hair, whose mouth curved into a shy smile when those stormy eyes met mine. "You must be Henry," he said, before I could introduce myself. He offered me a hand I never wanted to let go. "Betty's told me all about you."

Betty. My sister. Who thought I should spend the day with her current beau, checking up on him instead of checking him out. My voice croaked, each word a sentence as final as death. "Jim. Yes. Hello."

I vowed to keep a distance between us but somehow Jim worked through my defenses. He had a quick laugh, a quicker grin, and an unnerving way of touching my arm or leg or bumping into me at odd moments that caught me off guard. He skirted a fine line, too nice to be just my sister's boyfriend but not overtly flirting with me. Once or twice I thought I had his measure, thought I knew for sure which side of the coin he'd call, but then he would be up in the air again, turning heads over tails as I held my breath to see how he would land. That first afternoon was excruciating—lunch, ice cream afterward, a walk along the boulevard as I tried to pin him down with questions he laughed off or refused to answer. I played it safe, stuck to topics I thought he'd favor, like how he met my sister and what he planned to do now that he was out of high school. But his maddening grin kept me at bay. "Oh, leave Betty out of this," he told me at one point, exasperated. "I know her already. Tell me more about you."

I didn't want to talk about myself. There was nothing I could say that would make him fall for me instead of Betty, and I just wanted the day to be over. I didn't want to see him again, didn't want to *think* about him if I could help it, and in my mind I was already running through a list of excuses as to why I couldn't attend my sister's wedding if she married him, when Jim noticed a matinee sign outside the local theater. "You like these kind of movies?" he wanted to know. Some creature flick, not my style at all, but before I could tell him we should be heading back, Jim grabbed my elbow and dragged me to the ticket window.

Two seats, a dime apiece, and he chose one of the last rows in the back of the theater, away from the shrieking kids that threw popcorn and candy at the screen. He waited until I sat down, then plopped into the seat beside mine, his arm draped casually over the armrest and half in my lap. "Do you bring Betty here?" I asked, shifting away from him. Better to bring my sister up like a shield between us, in the drowsy heat and close darkness of the theater, to remind me why I was there. Betty trusted me, even if I didn't trust myself.

Jim shrugged, uninterested. As the lights dimmed and the film began, he crossed his legs, then slid down a bit in the seat, let his legs spread apart until the ankle rested on his knee. His leg shook with nervous energy, jostling the seat in front of him and moving at the edges of my vision, an annoying habit, distracting, and when I couldn't stand it any longer, I put my hand on his knee to stop it. As if he had been waiting for me to make the first move, Jim snatched my hand in both of his, threaded his fingers through mine, and pulled my arm into his lap. "Jim," I whispered with a slight tug, but he didn't seem to hear me and didn't release my hand. I tried again—he just held on tighter, refused to acknowledge that I wanted him to let go. Leaning closer so I wouldn't have to raise my voice, I tried again. "Jim—"

He turned and mashed his lips against mine in a damp, feverish kiss. *I shouldn't*, my mind started, then *I can't*, then *Betty*. Then his tongue licked into me, softer than I had imagined and so much sweeter than a man had the right to be, and I stopped thinking altogether. I was a whirl of sensation and every touch, every breath, every part of my world was replaced with Jim. *Betty isn't getting him back*; that was my last coherent thought before I stopped fighting him and gave in.

Later that evening, my sister was waiting when I finally got home. "Well?" she wanted to know.

I shrugged to avoid meeting her steady gaze and mumbled, "Do you really think he's right for you?"

"Me?" she asked with a laugh. "Not at all. But Henry, isn't he just perfect for *you?*"

From the kitchen, I hear Jim come down the stairs. He opens the front door and I force myself to stay at the stove, fighting the urge to check on him. I wait, head cocked for the slightest sound—somewhere outside, an early bird twitters in the morning air and further away, a lawn mower roars to life. Only when I hear a shuffled step do I call out. "Jim?"

No reply. Dropping the spatula into the pan of scrambled eggs,

I wipe my hands on a nearby towel and move toward the doorway as I try to keep the panic from my voice. "Jim, that you?"

Before I reach the hall, the door shuts quietly. When the lock latches, I let out a shaky breath and pray, *Thank you*. Then I see him at the foot of the stairs, thumbing through a small pile of mail I left stacked beside the phone. The way he lifts each envelope makes me sad, and I force a smile to combat the frown that furrows his wrinkled brow. "Bills," I tell him. "Breakfast's almost done. Did you get the paper?"

He glances up at me with blank eyes and my heart lurches in my chest. Then recognition settles in and he smiles. "Henry," he says, as if to remind himself who I am. I nod, encouraging. "The paper? No. Did you want me to?"

"Didn't you go out to get it?" I ask gently. At the confusion on his harried face, I shake my head. "Never mind. Go sit down, I'll get it for you."

"I can—" he starts.

I pat his shoulder as I move around him toward the door. "I've got it. Have a seat."

It's only when I'm on the stoop, digging the paper out of the roses, that I remember the stove is on. "Jim?" I holler as I shut the door behind me. I hate that I'm like this—I know I should trust him but I can't. If anything happens to him, it'll be my fault because I know I need to be more careful, he needs me to watch out for him. I imagine him by the stove, the sleeve of his robe brushing across the heating element, unnoticed flames eating along his side... "Jim, where—"

The kitchen is empty. The eggs sizzle in the pan where I left them and I turn the burner off before they get too hard. In the dining room, a chair scrapes across the floor: Jim sitting down. Without comment, I gather up the plates and silverware I had set out in the breakfast nook and carry them into the other room.

Jim sits at the head of the long, polished table where we rarely eat, but he gives me a smile when I hand over the newspaper, and as I place a plate in front of him, he catches me in a quick hug. He sighs my name into my belly, his arms tight around my waist, then rests his head against my stomach and wants to know, "What's for breakfast?"

I don't have the energy to tell him again. "It's almost ready," I promise, extracting myself from his embrace.

My parents always called Jim *Betty's friend*, right up until the day she got married to someone else. By then the two of us had an apartment together, and at the reception my mother introduced us as simply, "Henry and Jim." Not *friend* or *roommate*, just Jim—in those days, no one felt compelled to define us further. My mother treated him like one of the family when we visited, and that was all I wanted. Let her believe we slept in separate bedrooms, if that's what she needed to think to welcome him into her home.

We bought this house in '64; the market was good and the realtor didn't question both our names on the mortgage. Jim was in college at the time, working nights at the packing plant just to pay his half of the bills. We had plans for the house—I wanted a large garden and Jim loved to swim, but we didn't have the extra money to sink into landscaping yet; we couldn't afford the house most months, let alone flowers and an inground pool. I had a job in marketing and spent most of that first year in the house waiting for Jim to come home. Sometime after midnight he'd stagger through the door, weary from standing on his feet all evening, clothes and hands and face black with grime and soot. I hovered in the doorway of the bathroom, watching the dirt and soap swirl away down the drain as he washed up. Some nights he sat on the closed lid of the toilet seat, pressed the palms of his

freshly scrubbed hands against his eyes, and struggled not to cry
from mere exhaustion. "I can't do this much longer, Henry," he
sobbed, my man reduced to a child by the weight of his world. I
knelt on the floor and gathered him into my arms, ignoring the
stench of sweat and oil that rose from his soiled clothing. He slid
off the toilet and into my lap as he hugged me close. Hot tears
burned my neck where he buried his face against me. "I can't,"
he whispered, hands fisting in my clean shirt. "I just can't."

I helped when I could, but times were hard for us. Many
nights we sat together on the floor of the bathroom, me smoothing my hand along his back as he railed against it all. It was
college that held him back, Jim believed—if he could just drop
the few classes he took, he could work full-time at the plant and
make more money, but I wouldn't let him. In those days a degree
guaranteed a good paying job, no matter what the field of study,
and I knew Jim wanted to be more than a line worker the rest of
his life. I wanted him to be something more—I wanted him at a
day job and home in the evenings, in the bed beside me at night.
He wanted it too, so he would cry himself out as I held him, but
eventually he kissed my neck and whispered my name. "How
are you feeling?" I'd want to know.

With a shaky sigh, he would admit, "Better."

One evening I was in the kitchen, washing the dishes, when
I heard him come in the front. "Jim?" I called out, raising my
voice above the running tap. The slam of the bathroom door
was his only reply. Shutting off the water, I dried my hands and
glanced at the time—barely eight o'clock. My first thought was
that he had managed to get off early somehow, but the slammed
door made me worry. In the hallway, I knocked on the bathroom door. "Jim? You in there?"

"Be right out," he promised.

Absently my hand strayed to the doorknob but when I tried

to turn it, I found it locked. That bothered me more than I cared to admit—there were no locked doors between us. "Jim?" I asked again, twisting the knob in a futile gesture. I wanted to watch him get cleaned up, to see the man emerge from beneath the sooty worker, to watch his strong hands smooth over one another to wash dirty suds away. It had become a nightly tradition of sorts, and I saw so little of him as it was. With my ear pressed against the door, I could hear water and Jim's low humming. "Open the door," I told him and then, because that sounded too harsh, I added, "Are you all right?"

He hollered back, "Fine, Henry. I'll be right there."

I couldn't shake the feeling that something was off, so I stood outside the bathroom door and ran through a dozen scenarios in my mind, reasons why Jim would refuse to let me see him before he got cleaned up, but none of them made any sense. I couldn't imagine what he might be hiding from me, why he needed to wash up alone; there was no reason for the impromptu shower I heard running on the other side of this locked door. Never one for waiting, I wedged myself against the doorjamb, knob gripped tight in my sweaty palm. As soon as the shower cut off, I started rattling the knob again. "Jim—" I started, but then the lock disengaged and the knob turned in my hand. "What's all this about?"

He wasn't standing on the other side of the door, so I eased it open and peered behind it. Jim leaned back against the counter by the sink, a bath towel around his shoulders that barely covered his crotch. His legs, damp and swirled with dark curlicues of wet hair, stretched out for miles beneath the towel. One corner of the towel was caught between his teeth, and he stared at me with wide eyes full of an anticipation that excited me. "Well?" I wanted to know. I tried hard to hang on to my sour mood but the sight of water beaded on so much bare skin made it hard to remember what it was I might be angry about. "What's going on?"

Without replying, Jim scooted over. On the counter behind him sat a potted bush in full bloom. Salmon colored rosebuds peeked through thick green leaves, one or two in full bloom like bubblegum bubbles, their petals opening to a deep, gorgeous color that reminded me of hidden flesh. "Jim," I started, but I couldn't think of anything else to say. I had done enough window-shopping at the local nursery to know the plant must've cost a pretty penny. I wanted to ask how he could afford it, with tuition on the rise and the bills we had piling up, but I tamped that down and took a tentative step toward the counter. "It's beautiful."

"It's for you," Jim said. His eyes flashed above an eager grin he hid behind the towel. Before I could thank him, he added, "You know why?"

I brushed my fingers across one velvet petal and shook my head. "I can't begin to imagine," I murmured. My birthday was months away. Burying my nose into an open rose, I breathed deep the flower's heady perfume and sighed. "Did you get a raise? Did you graduate?" With a sidelong glance, I teased, "We didn't have a fight this morning, did we? Am I forgetting something?"

Jim laughed. "It's sort of our anniversary," he said, watching me, waiting for it to click.

It didn't. "Which one?" I ticked them off on my hand, one finger for each occasion. "We got the apartment in August, bought the house in February, first had sex in June, first kissed in..." A slow smile spread across my face. "In May. This is the day we met, isn't it? God, how long as it been?"

"Ten years today," Jim admitted. To the roses, he said, "They say red means love but these were the prettiest ones they had. I thought you'd like them—"

"I love them," I said simply, then gave him a smoldering look and added, "I love you. Come here."

He stepped toward me, away from the counter, and my hand brushed his arm before slipping beneath the towel to smooth over warm, tight skin. The towel fell away; Jim fumbled with the zipper of my pants, his hands undressing me as my mouth closed over his. We held on to each other as we met in a heated clash of lust and desire—against the wall, on the counter, sprawled across the lid of the toilet seat before we fell to the floor, aching and hard and seeking release. "I love you," I told him, again and again. I kissed the words into the hollow of his throat, the small of his back. I whispered them in his ear, then licked after them as he gave in to me.

Time has banked the fire that once burned so brightly between us. It still simmers just below the surface of our lives and occasionally flares at a word, a touch, a smile, but we are no longer the hot lovers we were before. When we make love now it's a gentle affair, languid and slow, the movements careful like turning the crumbling pages of an ancient book. Most evenings we settle for lying close together, Jim's arms around me, my body clutched tight against his. There will come a time when one or the other of us finally lies alone, maybe sooner than we care to think, and the thought of going on without him terrifies me. I've lived with him for so long now that I can't imagine anything else. So I smooth over his forgetfulness, these little spells that seem to come more frequently now, and I tell myself I can take care of us both. If ever the day comes when he wakes beside me and my name doesn't come to his lips, when that bewildered look in his eyes doesn't fade away, I'll remember for us both. I won't let him forget the life we built together. I won't let him go.

In the kitchen, I scrape the congealed eggs into a large bowl and stir them up to keep them fresh. If we were eating in the breakfast nook like I had planned, I wouldn't have to make several trips to deposit everything onto the table, but Jim chose the dining room and I give him an encouraging smile when I set the bowl of eggs down in front of him. "Help yourself," I say over my shoulder as I head back into the kitchen for coffee that's just beginning to perk. I busy myself with buttering toast, then rescue two overcooked sausages from the stove where I left them. When I bring the bread and meat out, I notice that Jim hasn't touched the eggs yet. "Everything okay?" I ask him.

He takes the plate of toast from me with one hand—the other is under the table, out of sight. I wonder if he's burned himself on the stove earlier while I retrieved the paper or maybe on the bowl of eggs; that ceramic gets pretty hot. But he gives me a quick grin and a flash of the boy I fell for peeks out through the face of the old man I love. "Everything's fine, Henry. You worry too much. You always have. Do I smell coffee?"

"Coming right up." I hurry back to the kitchen to pour two steaming mugs, with a dash of milk and a spoonful of sugar in Jim's because that's the way he likes it. I take mine black. As I blow across his mug to cool it off, I wonder what the rest of the day will bring. Will it turn out all right in the end? Or will this be one of those bad days, with Jim locked in the past, unable to follow my conversations because he can't remember one moment to the next? Some days he's a different man, aged by forgetfulness that borders on something I'm afraid to admit, much older than me despite the fact that I'm five years his senior. Since the scare at the front door, I'm on guard, suspicious and cautious and hating myself for not being able to trust him.

Back in the dining room, Jim holds the newspaper open in front of him, hiding from me. I'm about to ask him to lower it when I see the single rose on my plate. The flower isn't in full bloom yet, but all the thorns have been broken off and the long stem is ragged at the end, as if plucked in haste. Already the soft petals that peek through the green have that deep pink of young, forbidden skin. One of my roses...

My hands begin to tremble and I have to set the mugs down before I spill the coffee. It's May already, I should have remembered—when I close my eyes, we're both young again, awkward with sudden desire, each desperately waiting for the other to make the first move. In the darkness of my memory I recall that first fumbling kiss and the hot hands that held mine in his lap. The years between us peel away like the petals of a rose and the day we met is laid bare, the core around which we have built this life together. My vision blurs and I have to blink back an old man's tears as I finger the barely budding rose. "Jim," I sigh.

The paper rattles and I know he's trying to hide that grin of his from me. When I push down the top of the newspaper, he smiles as he says, "Of all the anniversaries we celebrate, you always forget this one."

"You always remind me," I point out. I can tell by the laughter dancing in his pale blue eyes and the promise in his smile that today is going to turn out to be a good day after all.

THE EMPIRE ROOM

Dale Chase

I look past the buffet table, out onto Jack London Square where tourists and pigeons wander. The scene offers escape from the mourners behind me. They're seated at large round tables and standing in little groups because Richie Knox, who was just thirty-six, killed himself a week ago and they're here to share a collective guilt. Mine's a tad worse because something untoward has begun.

I'm fixed on the Barnes & Noble across the square when he steps into view: Frank Bremer, Richie's friend. I met him an hour ago at the memorial service when Lisa, Richie's sister, introduced us. It began then, one of those moments that define life, make it worthwhile, or in this case, impossible.

He's gone outside for a cigarette. I watch him light up, tell myself that's reason enough to resist. I can't stand smoking. He paces while he drags on the thing. Clad not in a suit like the rest of us, he's chosen navy slacks, white shirt, and blue patterned vest. Too casual but on him it works. He's imposing, good looking, intensely masculine. Everything will depend on what he does with the cigarette butt. If he tosses it with no concern about litter, it's over. I wait while he paces and puffs, note his brown hair is a shade lighter in the sun. At last he turns, flicks the butt into a clump of shrubs where there are probably countless others, and I relax for a second because it's done. But then he comes back into the Empire Room and I know that's not the case.

We avoid each other. Like married people who know they're going to have an affair, we maintain a distance. He's gone over to Estelle, Richie's mother, my aunt, and is kneeling before her. Lisa comes up with a guy she introduces as Phil, Richie's business partner. I know from her call last week that Phil found Richie splayed in a living room chair, gun on the floor, brains all over. I shake Phil's hand, we speak, and I try to give myself to the moment but it doesn't work because I can look over Phil's shoulder and see Frank. The vest accentuates his build. It's tight, like maybe he's gained a few pounds. I look at his butt, then back at Phil; try to concentrate, do penance for impure thoughts. I work at listening but when Phil pauses I'm lost because I'm not taking in what he's saying. I'm in a kind of pleasure hell, like getting an erection in church. I excuse myself, hurry to the men's room, find only on reaching it that I do have to pee.

Who is Frank really? I wonder as I go. We'd spoken briefly but you don't get details with the casket ten feet away. Awful. Terrible. But in with such things the unmistakable energy. I remember my amazement that it was happening there, disgusting arousal. God help me.

I'm left to speculate, which is not good right now. There's enough of that going on about the suicide, how we could have missed it coming. We. I live four hundred miles away in L.A. but still apparently bear a portion of responsibility, even though Richie and I seldom talked anymore. Close as kids, our connection failed with distance and other priorities. I saw him holidays when the family gathered at Estelle's, if I chose to come north. I know he'd had a partner for several years, Tony, but they broke up. Tony's here. The question is how did Frank know Richie? So many degrees of friendship. Friend. Fuckbuddy. Lover. Former lover. Is he the reason? Part of the reason? Suicide is often about an accumulation of causes with one trigger, literally in this case. Was it Frank? He looks like someone you could die over but how am I to know? Not here. Not here.

As I leave the bathroom I almost run into him. "Sorry," I say automatically, then feel the rush he brings on. I let it run through me, familiar ache in with the unfamiliar. The worst kind of mix.

"Listen," he says but there is nothing more. Prelude going nowhere.

"Yeah, it's okay," I tell him. I look down as if even that much is wrong, shake my head because we're already into familiarity even when we're trying not to go there. Nature doesn't listen, does she?

We stand there because proximity feels good and we are both in need of feeling good but we catch it before it gets a grip. He sighs, moves past. I stand in the hallway, stunned all over again.

Leaving would solve it but it's too early. Nobody is leaving yet. I have to talk and eat and commiserate. Back in the Empire Room I listen to the hum of conversation, amazed at the quiet voices when we're all so pissed at Richie for doing what he did. Didn't he know the hole he'd leave? I watch Lisa coax her mother to eat. Estelle shakes her head. She lost her husband a year ago, now her son. Thank god for Lisa.

Frank gets a drink, goes out into the restaurant where a patio leads to the waterfront. I get as far as the door before stopping myself. I'm watching him when Ray, another friend of Richie's, comes up alongside, suggests we go out there. "Fresh air," he says, but I can't go because if I do I'll want to be alone with Frank so we can say what we know, act on it or make plans to act.

"No thanks," I tell Ray and he moves past. I see him talking to Frank, wonder if they have a history. I don't know enough about Richie anymore. It makes things worse, not having kept up. Funny because he pegged me early on when we were kids in Berkeley. Even at fourteen he was sharp, managed to start a conversation about girls, turn it to boys, and out first me, then himself. I'd told nobody but I told him everything and from then on, for two years at least, we were incredibly close. But then college and L.A. and life got between us and even the emails eventually thinned. Caught up in ourselves, we let the bond fray. Cousins was all that was left.

I cannot imagine him doing what he has done. They say he poured a drink and sat in his favorite chair, then put a bullet into his temple. Only Lisa knew he was depressed. He made her promise to tell no one and she kept that promise. He didn't want us to worry. He was seeing a shrink, was on meds, had a raft of people who loved him, none of it enough. I can't imagine letting go like that after all the fight we had in us.

Back inside I see Ted Quinn, the family dentist who came onto the scene two years ago when old Doc Felcher retired and sold him the practice. I saw him professionally last Thanksgiving thanks to a walnut shell in Aunt Estelle's special apple-walnut stuffing. He'd fixed me up with a temporary crown and we'd had sex that night. I'd lied to the family, said I had to get back to L.A. when all I did was spend the long weekend at Ted's house high in the Berkeley hills. I hadn't seen him since.

As he makes his way toward me everything falls into place. He got involved with Richie, threw him over and caused the suicide. Ted's a powerhouse but it's all on his terms. Richie wouldn't have had a chance.

"Carl, good to see you," he says, extending a hand. "Awful about Richie. I'm so sorry."

I know it's the usual line but I take it otherwise. He's sorry he killed him. Fury rises but gets sidetracked when he asks me how long I'll be in town. I consider making the date because fucking sounds good right now and having a history makes it not so wrong. "I'm flying out tomorrow morning," I tell him.

"Any plans for later?"

I smile, shake my head, look away.

"Okay," he says, "so maybe this isn't the appropriate time to ask, but I'd really like to see you. We had a great time last year."

Do it, I tell myself. *Go fuck 'til you drop. It'll make you forget Richie.* I'm ready to concede but when I look up I see Frank coming back in and everything else disappears. Even Richie. Ted for sure. "I don't think so," I say, looking past him.

"Your loss," he snaps before moving on.

Frank has caught me looking and comes over. I allow it because Ted got something started.

"This is so awkward," Frank says. I'm near the buffet. He picks up a cracker, turns it over, examines the back, picks at it with his thumbnail. His discomfort mirrors mine and I almost laugh when that hits me. We are not going to win. When I look into his eyes I see the invitation and in my hesitation he has to see acceptance. Let's go get a room. But we stand paralyzed.

"Shit," he says, tossing the cracker onto the table before walking away. I think I've lost him then, endure an anguish until Marie, Lisa's best friend, catches him by the arm and starts to talk. She's single and hasn't a clue about Frank. She slips her arm through his, guides him to the bar where I watch the buy-me-a-drink routine.

I haven't cried for Richie, and wonder if I ever will. I spoke at the service, told how we were as kids, but unlike Tony and Lisa and Phil, never shed a tear. Suddenly I feel it come up, a rift tearing through me like some rupturing fault line. Jagged edges, plates misaligned; I see us as kids with our dicks out. We sucked each other, a first for both. I can't believe he's dead. I look for a place to look, find a basket on the buffet table, silverware inside a cloth-lined dark brown weave. I concentrate on the folds in the fabric, the way it lies askew, and I decide that's how everything is now, off kilter. Tears are on my cheeks, my throat tightening. God, Richie, how could you do such a thing? How could life be that bad?

My stomach starts to churn and I flee, out of the Empire Room, out the front door, through the square, down alongside the boats. Cold air slaps me and I suck in a chest full. People are here, happy people gawking at the water, and I hate them because they keep on when it all should stop. I hurry along the quay toward container cranes that loom like giant four-legged beasts and only when I stop do I realize Frank has followed me. He touches my sleeve and I start to cry, fall into his arms. "Let it go," he soothes. "Let it go."

I do just that, shudder and sob as he holds me. "Tighter," I tell him and he adjusts his grip, holds on until I start to hiccup. "Oh, god," I say, pulling back. He hands me a handkerchief. I mop up.

We stand side by side looking at the ocean. "He took part of me with him," I say when the hiccups stop. "I didn't know it until just now. There's a history only he knew and in a way that's gone too. How could he do it?" My voice escalates in volume, my hands shake as they grip the iron railing. "How could he?" I demand.

"He made a choice and we have to respect it," Frank says.

"An awful choice but it was his to make."

"And nobody else matters."

"I doubt he thought of it that way. He had to have been in a lot of pain to do what he did. It was bigger than all of us put together."

"Self-centered little shit."

Frank chuckles. "You know better than that."

He's right of course but instead of getting me refocused on Richie, he's made me wonder about him. "How did you know him?"

"We met two years ago when his company came in to fix our computer problems. You know how he was, personable, absolute genius with computers, great listener. Everyone loved him and he did a great job. We hit it off right away, found we both liked mountain biking. For the last two years we've biked up Mount Diablo every Saturday morning, rain or shine."

"I hadn't seen him since Thanksgiving," I offer. "He seemed fine then, just bought the condo, was hiring more employees, totally up."

"Depression isn't a constant," Frank replies. "Every time I saw him he seemed happy, full of energy. Even with the biking he still went to the gym three times a week."

Memories of now push me back to memories of then. I go all the way back. "I remember being six, in a wading pool with him, trying to sink toy trucks."

Frank sighs, looks up at the idle cranes. A couple of inches taller than me, heavier but solid. Attractive. And he knows what's going on in me because he says, "We weren't involved, it didn't work that way between us. We were just good friends."

I nod because this clears the way, or at least it's supposed to. I start to cry again. "I can't do this," I tell him. "But god I want to."

"I know."

"Okay, then," I say and I walk away because that's all that's left. Back inside I feel suddenly exhausted. I'd gotten the call Monday, was told about services on Thursday, flew up Friday. It's Saturday now, one week to the day since Richie did it. It's been him all week and the vise that clamped onto my gut when I got the news hasn't let go. I nibble a bit of cheese from the buffet. It is tasteless. I chew and swallow, get a glass of wine at the bar.

People are starting to leave. I see them talking to Estelle who barely speaks. Her gray curls nod. She wants this done more than any of us. I want to leave but can't bring myself to do the necessary good-byes so I sit at an unoccupied table, allow the fatigue to wash over me. I think about later, back at Lisa's, wish I'd gotten a hotel room. I think about the plane tomorrow, how I'll remain silent for the one-hour flight.

Tony comes over, sits down. His eyes are red and puffy. "I'll never get over him," he tells me with a heaviness I understand. Tony is younger, maybe twenty-five. I know it was hot and heavy between them for several years. Richie wouldn't talk about the breakup.

"What happened with you guys?" I ask. My tone is accusatory. I don't care.

"I wanted to be exclusive and he didn't. The whole time we were together he saw other people. I finally couldn't stand it."

I think of Frank. Was he "other people"? I can see them going up Mount Diablo on their bikes, sweaty after the ride, getting it on at the summit then riding back down and life goes on. It makes me hate the arrangements of life, the need to take up with people on different levels.

"I was so in love with him," Tony says when I offer no comment. "God, this is agony."

Part of me wants to offer consolation but it's too small a part, buried under everything else. Frank is at the bar talking to people I don't know. I stare openly at the back of him, not listening to Tony anymore. I gulp my wine, hope it will loosen something in me, anything in me. Tony gets up, walks out of my periphery.

Andy, Lisa's husband, sits down beside me. "You okay?"

"I have no idea."

"Yeah, it's rough. If there's anything we can do or if you just want to talk, we're here for you."

"Thanks." I've heard this line from everyone I know and for a second they all run together and I'm back in my life in L.A. and Tim and Mark and Paul and Marcy are all saying it over and over. It bounces off me, rolls down my sleeve. Andy pats me, gets up, moves on. I look down as if there will be residue. Then movement catches my eye. It's Frank shaking hands, making the rounds as he prepares to leave. I feel numb as I see him talk to Lisa, Andy, Phil, Estelle. He's wonderful with my aunt. His hand on her cheek pierces me, lets my last breath escape. I sit absolutely deflated, watch as he rises from her and turns to go.

I wait for him to look at me but he doesn't. He strides out the door into the main hall and I feel a hundred things, urgency and desperation uppermost. But I also feel paralyzed, weighted. He disappears and I let the loss roll over me, feel my bones crunch. But when I finally raise my head I catch sight of him out front lighting a cigarette and I let out an involuntary cry. And I get up and without saying good-bye to anyone I go out to him.

COMING HOME

Shanna Germain

It's the first time I've been home in four years and no one seems to be around. I'm a day early, but it's odd to come up the long driveway and find the house and barns quiet. Even the horses are hidden from view, probably down in the low pasture taking shelter under the apple trees.

The only thing that looks occupied is the big hay barn. The door is open and a green T-shirt hangs from the water pump handle. It's haying time, so likely my stepmom hired whatever teenage football hero they could find to help stack. A football hero's ass is as good a diversion as any around here, so I head that way while I wait for the family to come back.

I walk through the grass, loving the way it reaches up and touches my feet around my sandals. Whatever my dad and stepmom think of me living in the city, however much I defend it when I talk to them on the phone, I miss the farm, the way it connects me with the truth. You spend enough damn time in the city and you think the world is made of concrete and pretty boys who like to suck your dick and buy your art. You forget the world isn't like that at all; the world is like this: slanted summer sun in late July, the sweet scent of clover and first-cut hay, a walk across shaded grass from house to barn.

Inside, the barn's hot. That's something you don't forget, how the heat comes through the walls and off the bales of hay and into your skin. It smells like yellow sunshine and the tang of sweat from whoever's throwing bales up in the loft. A memory stirs in the back of my mind, tries to harden into something, but I push it away. I pull myself hand-over-hand up the rickety ladder and hoist myself onto the wooden floor of the hayloft.

And then I'm face-to-ass not with some high school boy whose butt I can secretly ogle while he stacks bales. No. I'm face-to-ass with my stepbrother, who I haven't seen since the day I left here.

That's his green T-shirt down on the pump. I try not to stare at his bare back, the dotted line of his spine, the way his lats wing out when he picks up a bale of hay. Just these few years have widened and flattened him, given him the broad shoulders of someone who does manual labor for a living. His forearms are wiry muscle laid over bone, the kind of build you never find on city boys.

"Matt?" I say it like maybe it's not really him. Like maybe I can make him disappear if I say his name. Wishing in reverse.

"Yet," he says. Which in the language of the farm means, "yes." Or "who the fuck's asking?"

He turns. His hat shadows his face, but I can see the same spattering of freckles across his chin and cheeks, the same intense green eyes. Same color as uncut clover, as corn husks, as the best green grass that kisses your feet.

He heaves the bale he's holding against the far wall. It thuds against the others, sending up a shower of chaff. Dry dust coats my throat.

"What…" I swallow the scratch in my throat. "What are you doing here?"

Last I'd heard, he'd gone off to Wyoming or Montana or some-such. Looking for work on a real ranch. Not a two-bit pony farm like his mother owned. No one had mentioned anything about his being back.

"What's it look like?" He doesn't stop. Bale after bale. Sweat makes a dark semicircle above the ass of his jeans, and his skin is coated with so much moisture and green chaff it looks like he's been dipped in antifreeze.

I've been gone for four years. I thought it was safe to come home. I could visit, spend some quality time with Dad and my stepmom, ease the wounds that I inflicted when I left, abruptly, without explanation. I could come and then I could go back to the city, to the life I'd made. Not an amazing life, but a decent one. But no. Matt is here. My stepbrother is home and I don't know why.

He slides his fingers beneath the baling twine, heaves another bale, and I tell myself that I'm not staring at his ass and his thighs in his tight, worn jeans. I tell myself that I don't want to be that bale, fingered and tossed. I don't.

"Dad and…" I hesitate. I usually call my stepmom "Mom" but with Matt here, I can't say that. "They know you're doing this?"

"Asked me to." Matt finally stops moving. He's bigger when he's still. I have to take a step back, toward the edge of the loft, to make space for my breath.

Matt pulls a gallon jug of water from behind a bale and lifts it to his lips. His Adam's apple bobs while he drinks and I have the sudden taste of October in my mouth, his spit flavored with apples and whiskey. A vision of him naked, slim hips and hard cock bathed in the candlelight of pumpkin smiles. The scrape of my knees afterward, from kneeling on the concrete in my costume.

I shake the image away and focus on the sweat rolling down the back of my neck. A diversion. "Jesus Christ, it's hot up here." I fan myself by pulling the fabric of my T-shirt away from my chest.

"Yet," he says again. And this time, it doesn't mean anything close to yes. It means, "fuck you, city boy." And he's right to say it. He's probably been up here for hours. All I've done is climb the ladder.

He gestures with the half-full jug at my shorts and leather sandals.

"Gonna' work in those?"

"Wasn't planning on it." I realize I've dropped back into the language of the farm, words of thrust and grab. Half sentences and dangled meanings. You think you get away from it, but how quickly it comes back.

"Cut your pretty legs all to hell."

"Fuck you," I say, and then wish I hadn't.

He spits into the hay and tosses me a pair of leather gloves. I manage to catch them, more out of sheer determination than out of any skill. The scent of him fills the air—leather and tang and oil. The parts of me that are not breaking have hardened to stone.

"Fine," I say. I yank on the gloves and slap them together, hard. Matt grunts in response and holds out the water jug. I remember the taste of it: lukewarm water inside plastic, the salt of Matt's lips on the opening. If I took that jug, I would suck it like a man dying of thirst.

"No thanks," I say.

"You stacking or throwing?"

"Stacking." It's the wrong choice, the hard choice. But I have to take it.

"Good."

The hayloft's big, but it's half-filled with hay, and there's no way for us to get past each other without nearly touching. I fuck with my gloves as we pass, pretending they don't fit quite right. I look at Matt's work boots and I don't inhale as he goes by, like you might at a graveyard, until he is safely past and the ghost of him cannot get inside my mouth.

It doesn't work. My tongue prickles for his salt and sweat skin, my hands ache to feel those haying muscles pressed beneath them. I thought miles and years would be enough to save me. I was wrong. If he offered himself to me now, I could not say no. The only relief I have is that he will not offer.

I step in front of the wall Matt's been building and I lift the first bale. Bales are fucking heavy. You don't forget that either, but somehow I forgot what heavy meant. The first bale tears the shit out of the top of my thighs. "Mother fuck," I say as I swing it up and stack it. Matt doesn't look over; he just starts heaving bales in my general direction.

We work like that for a while, me swearing every other bale or so, the hay cutting into my tender skin, Matt throwing the bales long-ways across the barn to me like they're crabapples and not sixty pounds of clover. I stack the bales three, four high in time to Matt's grunt and their thud behind me.

We were, what, nineteen, last time we did this together? But just like the language, there's a rhythm here you fall back into. Roles that have been assigned, that you can't escape. Roles like stacker, thrower, brother, lover.

With my back to him, with the bales pressing against thigh and cock to keep things contained, I can remember. The first time, after his pony died and he hid himself up here, crying so softly no one could find him, but I did. And I held him until our mouths found each other and I tasted his salt tears, licked them from his cheeks and lips. That year the corn was tall enough to hide us, and my skin smelled like sweet, white corn for an entire summer. The last time, here, right here, between loads of hay, quick and hot, as if we knew it was our last, as if we were trying to hold something together that was already falling apart.

And then it *was* over. I told Matt I couldn't look my dad in the eye anymore, that I was tired of thirty-second blow jobs in the back of the tractor, of always watching over my shoulder. It was the only time I heard him say, "faggot." So much fucking contempt, the way he spit it out.

He wasn't talking about me.

I finish a row and step up on it to look out the high window. I can see the horses from here, standing in the shade of the apple orchard. The foals play-fight, rearing up with their baby teeth and hooves, instinctually preparing themselves for whatever the future might hold.

"You working or standing?" Matt tosses a bale, hard. It banks off the stacked bales and catches me in the side of the leg. My knee buckles, and I try to catch myself on the way down, but the only contact I manage is chin to bale. The stems rug-burn my cheek as I land.

I lie on the wooden floor, breathing heavily, waiting to see if any of the throbbing pain moves into something higher, something broken. The throbs stay steady and I push myself up to a sitting position.

"Christ, Matt," I say.

Matt steps toward me, head lowered. There's something in his eyes that I'm afraid to see.

"Damn," he says. "I didn't mean…"

Matt leans his hat back to wipe his brow with green-tinged fingers. His dark bangs are sweat-plastered to his forehead. The wrinkles across his forehead are lined with green sweat the same color as his eyes.

"You're bleeding," he says.

I look down; pinpricks of blood have popped up along my thighs.

"No, your face," he says.

It's not bad, just a dark smear on my fingers. Still, my arms shake when I push myself up. I pretend I don't notice Matt's hand, held out to help me. My legs are weak, wobbly.

"Let's just finish this," I say.

"We'll both stack," he says. " 'sfaster."

I nod. I reach down to pick up a bale. I throw it up, into the air, but it's heavy, too heavy, and I have to let it fall. The bale lands sideways, breaks apart a section of the careful wall I've built. Chaff darkens the air and makes it hard to breathe.

"Matt, fuck, why are you here?" I ask.

Matt stacks two more bales, forcing them to fit against each other, tight blocks of bodies pressed unwillingly together. The last one won't go, and he tries to hip-thrust it into place before he finally pulls it out, throws it down on the ground. His triceps muscle swells.

He looks at me from under the rim of his hat, clover eyes gone dark, and I'm afraid my knee's going to give again, just from the weight of his stare.

I reach for something to hold on to, but before I can, he answers.

" 'Cause I heard you were coming home."

And then my knees do give, both of them. Matt steps forward as I go down in the hay. His hand, his big, heavy hand, is gentle on my head. I lean my tender cheek to the front of his jeans, feel his hard heat through the fabric.

He joins me in the chaff until we're face-to-face, so close I can see the flecks of yellow that hide in his eyes.

"Was hoping it was true," he says. And I try to say that it wasn't true, that I'm not back, that this isn't home, but his lips are pressed against mine, and his tongue is telling me the truth.

THE BELT

Kal Cobalt

The suite door snicks shut behind Tobin. David sits in the chair. Tobin starts to sweat.

"How many times?" David's words are quiet, controlled. He's fully dressed.

Tobin's gaze drops to David's waist. Shit. The leather one. David owns a woven belt, something casual and textured that reminds Tobin of tennis players and doesn't hurt much. This is the serious belt. Its buckle gleams, the same silver as David's hair. It's an extension of David's body, of his aesthetic.

This is my flesh hitting you, David had said the first time, while Tobin sniveled on his knees, uncomprehending. *This is my tongue tasting you. This is my hand caressing you. This is my cock fucking you.* A new perspective for every sharp crack of the belt. David hadn't spoken about it after that first time. He hadn't had to.

"Tobin. How many times?"

Tobin drops to his knees just inside the doorway. How many

times today? He's always aware, at the time, that he's doing it, but somehow he forgets to count. "Fourteen?"

"No. Come here."

Tobin crawls. As he nears David's feet he lowers himself further, moving forward on forearms and knees till David's scuffed black shoes are directly beneath his chin. This close, he can feel David's heat, a strange, penetrating warmth like that of a few stiff drinks. David hasn't showered yet; he's stopped smelling like cologne and started smelling like a man.

"How many times?"

"Seventeen?"

"No." Beneath Tobin's gaze, David's feet move apart. "Take it off me."

Tobin shifts up enough to unfasten David's belt buckle, keeping his eyes lowered. The leather is warm from David's body, firm but supple, reminiscent of the animal it once was. Tobin had mentioned that once, carefully. *I merged with the animal,* David had said. *I took its skin for my own and impregnated it with metal, and now it is me. It's all very primal, Tobin. It's all very evolutionary.*

"How many times?"

"Twenty-one."

"No. Give it to me."

Tobin folds the belt in half and offers it up, his head down, as if presenting a sword to a king. His king. David accepts the belt slowly, then holds it in one hand so he can stroke Tobin's cheek with the other. Tobin keeps his eyes down, hot at David's touch.

"How many, Tobin?" David's voice is soft, to match the caress.

"Twenty-five," Tobin whispers, his throat thick with shame.

"No. Hold out your hands."

Keeping his head down, Tobin holds both hands out, palms up, and waits.

Waits.

Waits.

The first strike is against Tobin's left palm; he hears it more than he feels it until the sting settles in, deep and intense. "One, Master," he gasps, straightening his posture, holding his hands out flat once more. The second slap, Tobin thinks, is harder; it always feels like David strikes his dominant hand more sharply. "Two, Master," Tobin hitches out, resisting the urge to close his hands for even a moment.

"Breathe."

Respite. Tobin lets his hands drop slightly, careful to keep them open, and takes the opportunity to pull in a full breath and moisten his lips. He can feel David's impatience as they reach the end of the breathing time—its duration has never been spelled out, but Tobin feels it all the same—and he holds his hands up again.

It could be a stronger blow, or just the illusion of it after the break; either way, Tobin holds in a cry, waiting for the sharpest of the pain to dissipate before he trusts his voice. "Three, Master." How many times? How bad has he been? The guilt hurts almost as much as the next slap of the belt. He was very bad, very disrespectful, god knows how many infractions. "Four, Master." How he could do this, to his master, day after day, how he could forget the lessons his master crafts for him, so cruel and so clear…? "Five, Master." How many times? Tobin's palms ache, burn with his shame. How many more infractions? A dozen more? Two dozen more?

The leather strikes hard, cracking sharply against Tobin's skin. He hitches in breath to count off and can't find enough air to do it. Dimly, he realizes he's crying. It doesn't matter. He has to find the breath to speak, to answer and appreciate his master's punishment. He holds his hands up higher, a silent supplication for patience, and then breath comes back to him in a single shuddering gust. "Six," he sobs out softly, "Master." He wipes his nose on the shoulder of his shirt and holds position, waiting for the next slap.

"That's all."

David's voice is calm, velvet stretched over steel. Tobin blinks away tears, raising his head, looking up past the erection tenting David's unbelted pants and into his master's eyes.

"Only six," David murmurs. His expression warms a little, crow's feet deepening as affection reaches his eyes. "You're improving. I'm pleased."

"Thank you, Master." Tobin's voice is thick through his tears. He keeps his hands out, red, swollen; his master hasn't ordered anything different.

"Are you hard?" David nudges his foot between Tobin's thighs to find out for himself.

"Yes, Master."

"Undress."

Tobin gets to his feet just long enough to divest himself of everything but his shirt. That he can remove on his knees, and once it's off, he holds out his hands.

David passes his fingertips across Tobin's right palm, then his left. "Good boy. Now suck me."

Opening his master's fly is not an easy task; Tobin's hands are swollen and burning as he forces his fingers to work the button and zipper. David's erection is wide, pale, thickly veined, and Tobin wraps one hot hand around the shaft, squeezing though the motion drives sharp pins of pain along the lines where David's belt fell. Tobin licks his lips and takes the head of David's cock into his mouth, sucking gently, nursing at the very tip till David gives that first telltale moan of approval.

Tobin closes his eyes, heated through by the sound. It's here, when that sound of satisfaction rumbles free from David's throat

like the purr of a contented lion, that David transforms from his
master to his lover. David's hand comes up to caress the side of
Tobin's face, fingertips tracing the contours of Tobin's cheekbone as if it were some rare and delicate artifact, and Tobin
opens wider, relaxing his throat, taking David in to the root.

"Enough," David breathes. "Bed."

Tobin favors David's cock with one last sucking stroke, smiling lightly as he gets to his feet. David skins off everything but
his T-shirt, leaving black garments of various fabrics draped
over assorted furniture as he heads to the bedroom. It's a weak-
ness, that T-shirt. Tobin knows it, but only because David told
him, and as such it's a secret, a sacred and intimate thing Tobin
would never question. It's more me than I am, David had said. I
am alienated from my chest.

Tobin pulls back the covers, finds the faint stain from last
night's sex still present on the sand-colored sheets. It's a waste,
David says, to have the bedding washed nightly, and there is a
comfort to sleeping in one's own smell. That, too, Tobin has accepted without question, as he has accepted the knowledge that
stretching out under the covers, on his back, legs spread, is the
way David wants him every night.

There is no speaking, and after David climbs into bed and
rolls on top, there is no light. David's breath is warm and af-
fectionate at Tobin's cheek, pausing momentarily for kisses
along that same cheekbone; David's scent is dark and mamma-
lian, trapped by the sheets, as his thighs nudge Tobin's further
apart. Tobin reaches, blindly, and rests a hand on David's arm,
half over skin and half over T-shirt sleeve. When the lights are
on, David is always directing. In the dark, David trusts Tobin
enough to be himself.

A soft snap of plastic, a faintly moist, organic sound, and
David's hand is between Tobin's legs, spreading thick, viscous

lube. *To ease the friction,* David had said once, on a postcoital float between drags off the joint. *Like a well-functioning piston. Like oil in a car.*

David's fingers, then, well practiced in what Tobin can take. Tobin finds David's shoulder, clings to it, squeezes hard as David presses two fingers in, scissoring mercilessly. There are times when the foreplay is lengthy, times when David starts touching Tobin just after dinner and doesn't stop till they've passed out on the bed four hours later. Not tonight. Not on a correction night. Two fingers, scissored hard, and that's all; then David's shifting up to grab the pillow, and Tobin wets his lips, releasing a breath.

Tobin knows David's cockhead as intimately as he knows the pale crescent beneath David's right thumbnail, the slightly phlegmy stuttering throat-clearing David inevitably makes in his sleep forty-five minutes after he nods off, the way David needs his toiletries arranged just so on the bathroom counter. The tip of his cock is almost flat, and Tobin breathes out again, opening up to that familiar bluntness till he feels the flare at the base of the head slide into him. He knows the way the vein that runs across the top of David's cock is bulging right now; as David resists the primal urge to drive into Tobin to the root, Tobin knows the way David's buttocks tense, knows from the glimpse he had in a suite with a mirror once. The image comes back to him brightly in the dark, David's pale ass flexing, bracketed by Tobin's tanned shins.

David exhales, warm breath washing across Tobin's chest, and presses in slow and hard. Tobin moans, arching into it, reaching down to cup his cock. On the way there his fingers clash with David's, moving to do the same. There's a soft, short grunt of laughter from above, and Tobin smiles, groping for David's wrist and then pulling it down to his cock. Better David's hand than his.

David presses in again, passing his hand over Tobin's cock in a deceptively gentle motion. Tobin hitches his legs higher on David's thighs, then shifts them up to David's hips. The angle forces him to pull in a breath as David slides in another inch without even trying. David's moist fingers—lube? saliva?—find Tobin's nipple and squeeze, eliciting another moan that just keeps going as David slides all the way in.

David always rests, here, and Tobin reaches up to cup his hand over David's nape, breathing with him, finding the rhythm. *We merge,* David had whispered the first time, when he had cradled Tobin in his arms, fucking him hard and slow and so thoroughly Tobin could not even find the words to agree. *We merge like everything else. There is no singular being. Anywhere.*

Tobin shifts slightly, aware of the way David's weight begins to move, and then David's hand is on the mattress just beneath Tobin's armpit, bracing him. Tobin grips that upper arm, again half a hand of skin and half a hand of sleeve, and waits. David only starts when he's ready.

The first thrust is slow, learning the way their bodies fit together on this particular night. Tobin tips his hips up encouragingly, and David thrusts again, his breath catching. Tobin pushes his hips up, more forward this time, impatient. He knows what's coming. He doesn't want to wait. His cock is long and full against his belly, swollen and waiting for David's hand. All of Tobin is waiting.

David finds it, that nebulous *it* that slips him into his comfort zone, and the thrusts turn rough and jarring, forcing Tobin to link his ankles in an attempt to keep their bodies joined. David's breaths are harsh, focused, and Tobin reaches up to brace himself against the headboard, gasping as David's cock rubs him just so. David's free hand goes frantic then, clutching at Tobin's hip, then his shoulder, seeking just the right way to anchor

Tobin's body. Tobin works his hips up, fisting one hand in the front of David's T-shirt and yanking him closer, and that seems to do it. David cries out, a harsh, faintly startled sound, and his back arches sharply as he throws himself into Tobin for those final, crucial half-dozen thrusts. Tobin can feel David's semen jetting deep into him, and he moans; we merge, like everything else. There is no singular being. Anywhere.

David breathes, his forehead on Tobin's sweat-slicked chest. Closing his eyes, Tobin pets the back of David's T-shirt, damp and stuck to his skin with sweat. There is a transmutation that happens in these moments, Tobin has decided; there is a kind of magic that happens between when he accepts David's semen and when David coaxes his own out. The circuit is primed but not closed, and Tobin feels the whole of his being aching for completion, something far more basic and necessary than the urge to come.

David leans up and takes Tobin's cock in his hand, letting out a low murmur of pleased surprise at its state. It feels swollen in David's hand, distended like a pregnant woman's belly, as thick and filled with blood as his belt-whipped palms. David presses in again, his cock still half-hard, and Tobin sucks in a breath, waiting, again. Then David begins to stroke, long, tight passes Tobin knows intimately, as he knows the slow, languid grind David offers in counterpoint. Here, there is nothing but David; he is over and inside and all thoughts of a universe beyond him fade. David's hand tightens, working the top half of Tobin's shaft in a perfect squeeze-twist Tobin never taught him but David seemed to intuit, importing the motion from the endless lazy adolescent afternoons Tobin spent sprawled half-naked on his bed, employing the exact same technique till he'd milked himself dry.

Tobin gasps, arching his hips up into David's next press, and David quickens the pace of his hand, thumb working up the underside just below the ridge, over and over till Tobin tenses from head to toe, holding his breath till the orgasm breaks over him, forcing his cock up into David's hand again and again, semen hot on his belly as David strokes it out of him, easy at first, then with a firmer grip, seeking to squeeze it all out.

Drained, Tobin lies boneless, twitching sharply as David works the last of the semen from him. Then David's hand is on Tobin's thigh, and David gently pulls out; Tobin waits, eyes open in the dark, spent but waiting for that crucial closing of the circuit, so close now, David shifting lower and taking the sheets with him, David's breath warm against his cock.

There. David's tongue strokes Tobin's belly as he takes Tobin's semen, licking with a slow, concentrated methodology to make sure he finds it all. Tobin's skin cools where David's tongue has been, his saliva quickly chilling in the open air.

David moans, and Tobin relaxes; it's complete. David passes his hand gently over Tobin's belly as he shifts up and to the side, settling in against Tobin, and then, finally, is the kiss, thorough and quiet, David's hand at Tobin's nape, Tobin's hand at David's hip.

"I love you," David whispers in the dark, pressing his forehead to Tobin's.

Tobin had asked about that the first time, how love fit into David's mechanical, atheistic worldview. David had smiled, a coy little expression Tobin had rarely seen, and said: *I am a realist. I have experienced love, and therefore it exists.*

David takes Tobin's hand off his hip, brings it up to his lips, kisses the still-hot palm.

"I love you," Tobin whispers in return.

BOYFRIENDS: A TRIPTYCH

Shaun Levin

1. *The Cup of Vodka: A Fantasy*

A young man went cruising. He went to the park. He walked round and round until he came to a clearing he had never seen before. He went to the edge of the clearing. There was a beautiful man there, and when he saw the man he fell in love.

"I want to love you," he said to the beautiful man.

The beautiful man said: "How can I know that you are the one for me, a real man and the perfect boyfriend?"

The man said: "Try me in any way you wish."

So the man took a bottle of vodka from his pocket and filled a silver tumbler to the brim. "Here is a cup of vodka. Balance it on your head. Climb the apple tree at the far end of the clearing and bring me two apples from the top branch. You must not spill one drop of the vodka. Do this and I will be yours."

The man climbed into the tree. It was dark amongst the branches, but he noticed a small red light; someone was sitting in the tree, smoking. And he had his cock out. He was expecting some action. They smiled at each other.

The man in the tree whispered to the young man: "I've just heard what the beautiful man said." And he plucked a hair from his own chest, and put it into the cup. The vodka became solid, and the tumbler became fixed to the young man's head.

The young man climbed higher up the tree. He picked two apples from the top branch. On his way down, the man with his cock out was still sitting there. It was big and erect, and the young man touched it. "I'm tempted," he said. "But I'm in love." When he reached the ground, he took the hair from the cup. The vodka and the cup became as before. The young man walked up to the beautiful man and gave him the apples and the tumbler of vodka. The beautiful man said: "Truly you are a real man and perfect boyfriend material or you would not have done that thing without spilling one drop of the vodka."

The two men went home together in the beautiful man's beautiful car. They sipped vodka and ate apples all the way home. Then they had sex, and even came together. In the morning, the young man ate the breakfast the beautiful man brought him to bed. Later that week he moved in with the beautiful man and they are still living happily together.

2. A Misty Landscape with Glitter, Ice Cream, and Two Men: A Fatality

Paul met David in the steam room at Chariots. Paul had just been to a midweek barbecue where the children of the house had been sprinkling fairy dust on the guests. David had been to see some clients (he sold stationery) and popped into the sauna on his way home. He sat down next to Paul. He clearly liked hairy men. Their knees touched. David leaned over and took Paul's cock into his mouth. Paul liked a man with a voluptuous hunger. Men gathered round, the kind of crowd that gathers when two guys in a sauna are about to have sex—the older ones, afraid of rejection, watched; others, too beautiful to be touched, kept their distance.

Paul liked a masturbating audience.

When the heat became too much Paul felt his body had been drained of its liquids, and besides, what with sucking cock, having his nipples pinched, and the tongue of a short Spanish boy being shoved down his throat, he could hardly breathe. Paul left the steam room. David followed.

They stood on the threshold to the showers and kissed.

"There's glitter in your hair," David said.

They smiled into each other's mouths.

They were the opposite of each other. Paul was tall and stocky and hairy with an average-sized penis. David was slim and smooth, an inch shorter, but with an extra two inches to his cock. All the same, they were turned on by each other. After their showers, Paul suggested they find a cubicle, and led the way past the pool, down the stairs, then up to that row of three rooms with iron bars between them. Paul liked to be able to reach out and touch his neighbors.

They both felt special, cocooned in the intimacy they'd created. Men came to watch and tried to fondle them, but David pushed their hands away. Paul was more generous. At one point, a man with a very large penis—larger even than David's—knelt at the bars and jerked off while Paul fucked David. Paul took David's hand and put it on the man's cock.

After they came, Paul lay on top of David while they stroked each other.

"You're my blanket," David said, rubbing against the hairs on Paul's chest.

Paul felt he would do anything, be anything, to keep this man's hands on his back, caressing him.

"I'm going to have to go soon," he said, as if testing something.

"I won't let you," David said.

"We can't stay here all night," Paul said.

"You could take me home," David said.

When they got off the bus in Stoke Newington they bought a tub of Häagen-Dazs Strawberry Shortcake ice cream. The night air was cool and their steps were buoyant. Paul thought of the Michael Jackson video in which every square he stands on lights up. In bed, with a teaspoon, they fed each other ice cream, slowly, until David said he'd had enough.

"I'm getting fat," he said, and told Paul about his ex-boyfriend, a Lebanese guy called Kamal, whom he'd loved desperately and who left him when he became obese.

"By the time it was all over," David said, "I was fifteen stone."

"How did that happen?" Paul said.

"I got to a point where I just didn't care," David said. "I wasn't hardly doing anything, just eating and watching TV and having sex, and then we weren't even having that much sex. I was a pig."

"You look great now," said Paul.

"It's the Atkins Diet," David said. "And five days a week at the gym."

Paul imagined taking David home to meet his mother. He imagined dinners with his friends, and David's friends, one of whom was a painter. He imagined changing gyms, doing sit-ups together in the mornings. He imagined the new sign he'd put on his front door. He imagined moving to Enfield to live with David. Later, they'd buy a house together. He'd never been to Enfield.

They fell asleep in the spoon position.

In the morning they woke in each other's arms and had more sex. Paul was so turned on he thought his cock would never go soft.

"You're like a teenager," David said.

David made whimpering, gurgling noises when he sucked on Paul's nipples. It was a mixture of pleasure and a dread that the source of life would dry up.

"Keep making those sounds," Paul said.

Paul brought in chunks of fresh pineapple and made toast with peanut butter, which they ate in bed, naked. David called a couple of his clients and said he was stuck on the motorway, that he'd come in and see them later in the week. He told Paul about the stationery world. He said that Viking—where Paul got his stationery—was not giving him the best deal.

"They just offer free chocolates," David said.

Paul thought about "The Office" and about Ricky Gervais.

"When was the last time you had sex? Paul said.

"A couple of days ago," David said, and mentioned the pool table at Central Station, which, he said, smiling, he knew very well.

"How many guys?" Paul said, stroking the smooth crack of David's arse.

"Seven," David said.

"In a row?" Paul said.

"Well, five, actually," David said. "Two came back for more."

Paul liked men who took risks. He also thought about the kinds of diseases one could pick up in a place like that. He liked the idea of having a slutty stationery salesman for a boyfriend. After his last relationship, which had been stifling, he was ready to try the nonmonogamy thing.

"This is such a treat," David said, finishing his toast. "You're my treat."

"I must get up soon and do some work," Paul said.

He opened the curtains and let in the light. David was still beautiful and his eyes were bluer than they'd seemed the night before. Sunlight hit a speck of glitter on his shoulder. Paul thought of the ping on the tooth of a smiling mouth in an advert for dental care. He also thought that the sun on the skin of a man lying naked on a bed was a natural wonder. *Should I ask for his number,* Paul thought, picking up the tub of melted ice cream, drinking it, bits of shortcake dissolving in his mouth. He had no idea what David was thinking. So they got dressed and kissed at the front door. And that was the end of that relationship.

3. Their Way to You: A Happy Ending

Fred waited a couple of days, then on Thursday he called.

"Hello."

"Hi," said Fred.

"Hi," the guy said. His name was Michael. Fred knew this.

"You don't know me," Fred said.

"Yes?" said Michael. "Who do you want to speak to?"

"I saw you in Tinderbox a couple of days ago," Fred said.

"You what?"

"Tinderbox," Fred said. "On Upper Street. I saw you there with a friend."

"Where did you get this number?" Michael said.

"You gave it…" Fred said, filling his glass, walking back to the living room with the bottle and glass clawed between his fingers. "You gave it to the guy in the café. I heard you."

"You what?" Michael said. "I'm not sure I like this."

"Couldn't we just…"

"I'm going to put the phone down now."

Fred sat on the carpet and leaned against the sofa. He held

the phone to his ear until the dial tone was like an alarm clock at the far end of a room; he set the receiver back down.

"Hello."

"Hello," Fred said.

"Is that you again?" Michael said.

"I'm afraid it is," said Fred, on a Friday night, very drunk.

"I've got your number, you know," Michael said. "I did one-four-seven-one the last time you rang."

"Oh," said Fred.

"Don't call again."

"Hello."

"Hi," said Fred. "Please don't put the phone down."

"What?" said Michael.

"I saw you again today," said Fred. "In Highbury Fields."

"This isn't amusing," Michael said.

"Couldn't we just talk?" Fred said. He had nothing to fear.

"What are you doing this for?" Michael said, his voice deep and sharp, as if he had to project it over a great distance.

"I saw you jogging round Highbury Fields," Fred said.

"You what?"

"You know you keep doing that?" Fred said.

"What?"

"That," said Fred. "You say 'what' as if you hadn't heard what I said."

"Thanks," said Michael. "I'm glad you've pointed this out to me."

"I like the sounds of words," Fred said. "Are you training for the marathon?"

"What?"

"See?" said Fred. "Are you running the marathon?"

"Never again," Michael said.

"So, you've done it before," he said.

"What do you want?" Michael said.

"Look," said Fred. "I'm not mad. I saw you in Tinderbox, you were giving your number to a friend and I overheard. You were saying something about sensory perceptions in Aristotle. You're a good-looking guy."

"Oh, please," said Michael, his chuckle giving away way too much. "Are you desperate?"

"I fancied you, so I wrote it down," Fred said, thinking: *Isn't everyone desperate?*

"This is creepy," said Michael.

"Trust me," said Fred. "I'm not mad."

"How do I know that?" said Michael.

"Hello."

"Is that Frank Sinatra in the background?"

"It's the radio."

" 'My Romance'?" Fred said. "Is that Dinner Jazz?"

"Bingo," said Michael.

"You're cautious."

"Am I?"

Fred thought of quitting. Of saying: *I'm out of here.* But that would be like giving up; he couldn't walk out on something he'd started.

"Look, couldn't we meet somewhere?" he said. "I'm really bad on the phone. I hate it. I don't even have a mobile. I'm not sure what to say. I've made a fool of myself. Ask me something."

"Like what?"

"I don't know," Fred said. "Like: What do I do for a living? Have I got brothers and sisters? How tall am I?"

"So?"

"What?"

"Tell me."

"I'm a musician. I've got an older brother. I'm six foot two."

"What kind of a musician are you?"

"Piano" said Fred. "Tell me what you do."

"I write," said Michael.

"What?" said Fred.

"Stories."

"Cool," said Fred. "What kind of stories?"

"I don't have an answer to that," said Michael. "I suppose I should have one. Stories about life, I guess. I don't like that question."

"Why?"

"I don't. It makes me feel stupid."

"I'm sorry."

"Let's say I write stories about meaning," Michael said. "And relationships. And beauty. How does that sound?"

"Impressive," Fred said. "I wish I could create my own music."

"Yes."

"Don't pull away."

"Why?" said Michael. "Are you getting off on this?"

"No," said Fred.

"I'm sorry," said Michael. "What were you saying?"

"This is hard work. Not my ideal turn-on. But I do like you. I'm normal. If you saw me you'd see. Really. We could meet somewhere in public. Bring a friend to keep an eye."

"From behind a newspaper?" Michael said. "What's your name?"

"Fred."

"Are you serious?" said Michael. "As in Flintstone."

"Frederick J. Cohen."

"That's very distinguished."

"Just Fred is fine. What are you doing?"

"I'm sitting down. I've been pacing. Fred, hey?"

"And you're Michael."

"I am."

"Are you always hard work?"

"I think so," said Michael.

"Is that you, Michael?"

"Good voice recognition," said Michael.

"I was beginning to think you wouldn't call."

"Well, here I am."

"You're very defensive."

"This is not going to work. It's ridiculous. I hate it when people say they'll call and then they don't. Are you there? Fred? Let's just call it a day. Fred? Are you going to say something?"

"Hello?"

"You're very beautiful."

"Thank you."

"Your face is beautiful. They're deep blue, your eyes, aren't they? I wasn't that close. And that blush in your cheeks. Like a farmer, a mountain climber coming in from the cold. I love your hair. I wish I could touch your hair."

"You do, do you?"

"Those bouncy curls. I'd bob them in the palm of my hand. Did you turn the music off?"

"No."

"I thought the music stopped."

"It did."

"It's nice and quiet. Can I kiss you?"

"Is this phone sex?"

"Shh. Let me kiss you. Gently. Lie back and let me kiss you.

On your eyelids. Close your eyes. Let me kiss you there. Like this.
Softly. Don't open them. The right one. Like this. Your skin's so
soft against my lips. Now the other one. How does that feel? Let
me kiss your cheeks. Keep your eyes closed. Feel how dry my lips
are against your cheeks. Gentle pecks. Is that Barry White?"

"Mm," Michael said.

"I like him," said Fred. "You hardly hear him nowadays."

"Kiss me."

"Where?"

"Kiss me."

"On your lips?"

"Are you writing? Am I disturbing you?"

"It's okay."

"Did you get home okay?"

"Yeah, I took a cab from the station," Michael said. "I
couldn't be bothered with the Tube."

"Did you have money on you?"

"The driver stopped at a cashpoint," Michael said, and then
they were silent for a few seconds, a few delicious seconds, making room for Michael to say: "I'm sorry I didn't stay."

"That's fine," Fred said. "I wish you had. I liked cooking for
you."

"You're a good cook," Michael said. "And a good pianist."

"Thanks."

"Where did you learn to play like that?" said Michael.

"I'm not sure," said Fred.

"You must have started somewhere," said Michael.

"The official version is: one summer in Scotland, when I was
eight. We were staying in this castle, three families, for a month.
There was a piano in the drawing room. A pianette. One of the
fathers taught me, got me playing—but the keys were hard to

play; you had to bang on them to get them heard. It forbade meekness."

"I wish I'd had someone to encourage me to bang on the keys," Michael said.

"Your writing's loud," Fred said. "That's confidence."

"But it's all done in silence really," Michael said. "The world doesn't *hear* anything when I write, unless you're so close you can hear my pen scurrying across the page."

"I want to be that close," Fred said.

"Do you?"

"Is Fred there?"

"Just a sec. I'll get him for you."

"Are you busy?"

"Not really."

"Do you want to meet up for coffee? I could come to your place. Is everything okay? Are you okay?"

"No. My brother's still here, he's driving me mad. His wife doesn't want him, he's moping, and it's driving me crazy."

"I'll come to your end. We can walk through Camden. I need to get out. Get some exercise. Can I bring you another story?"

"So?"

"He's still here."

"Not him. So?"

"It's beautiful. I knew it would be."

"Thanks."

"How do you know all those things?"

"Like what?"

"About the army. War. Death."

"My dad was in the army, his father was in the War. My brother was killed in Bosnia."

"God."

"Yup."

"Michael?"

"It *was* you. I did one-four-seven-one. Are you okay? Michael? What's the matter? Mikey. Don't try and talk. I'm here."

"Should I tell you how he died?"

"Let me come be with you."

"They tortured him."

"I know. I know, sweetheart. I remember it from the papers. And the telly."

"Don't call me sweetheart."

"That's better."

"Stop being nice to me."

"But you are my sweetheart."

"I'm not. I'm horrible. I didn't see him for ten years, then he got killed, and now I'll never talk to him again. Never. Do you know what that means? Not ever in the world. I don't care if he was horrible to me. I don't. I don't care what he did to me. I want to talk to him. I want to talk to him about when we got lost in the woods in France and he found the way home."

"How?"

"He climbed a tree to look for rooftops. It was getting dark and he had this brainwave to follow the electricity cables. So we followed the outlines in the twilight until we got home. He was the best."

"Oh, Mikey. Sweetheart."

"I know."

"Do you want me to come over? I'll drive there. It'll take me half an hour."

"I'll be fine."

"You're so lovely."

"No, I'm not."

"Who's that?"

"Did you want to speak to Fred? Is that Michael?" she said.

"Yes?" he said.

"I'm Fred's mother," she said. "He told me about you."

"Oh," said Michael.

"He's just popped out to Sainsbury's. He'll be back in half an hour. Should I tell him to call you?"

"Yes, please. Tell him I called."

"Mikey?"

"Freddie."

"No, never Freddie. Were you on the phone now?"

"To your mother."

"Ah. Yes. I forgot it was Sunday lunchtime."

"But I've still not been fed my breakfast."

"I'm coming. I'm at the bakery counter. Chocolate or almond croissant?"

"Both. And coffee and strawberries and kiwi fruit."

"They're in the basket," Fred said. "On their way to you."

ENDLESS AGAINST AMBER

Matthew Lowe

Window down. The cool of an October night. Mad mile. How old were we? Sixteen? Seventeen? You, with your license since May. Me, with my hand out the window, dancing.

Black road ahead and us dipping and rising. Steady. Steady she goes. Taking the knocks like a boat to the waves. Music blaring from your new sound system. Tinny and wild. You. At the wheel, singing through your nose, tapping some crazy beat that didn't seem to go:

If this ain't love, why does it feel...why does it feel...so good?

Moonless night. Orange light beyond the trees, beyond the farms and the tangle of the wild sunflower. Broken free.

Better head home now. Time to turn back. Too late. Too light. Too much to handle in the morning. Believe me.

Just a little longer, a little further. Can't we just keep driving? Where the trees are dark and we could be anywhere.

Time has layers like an onion. The deeper you delve the more you must peel away. Layer upon layer...

I remember going worming on the mudflats with Adam Cooper. We'd dig trenches and draw up mud with pumps of PVC piping. Once, when we went trekking through the mangroves at low tide we found the skeleton of a dead turtle. Its shell like armor, its body all but washed away.

I used to cycle along the Esplanade with my dad. I remember "bring a bike" parties at Lota Park. We'd all drink Fanta and ride down to the wading pool for a swim.

And here's us at twelve, one Friday night at church youth group: me in the corner, contemplating my shoelaces; you in the middle, broad shouldered and bronzed, volleyball in hand.

Here we are crossing paths and you not looking. Here I am taking the Jesus-talk far too seriously. Here you are getting your first kiss behind the prickly hedges, and pretending like you'd done it all before.

Here's me seeing through it years later. Here's you not quite sure how to take me, but determined, discovering...

Did you know I thought you were a bully when I first met you? Did you know you and she together made me jealous?

Remember sitting there in my room? I remember telling you that I couldn't: "I've spent too much time with you now," I said, "you're too much of a friend to me." And you told me you felt the same.

You came and sat by me on the bed and our fingers touched and warmed. There was relief there and disappointment and something else—a film playing in an empty cinema, passions lost to a sea of seats.

I leaned in and kissed you.

Friday night. Escaping the olds and cruising the burbs. You and me in your rusty white hatchback, in the backstreets, in the half-light, holding off the dawn.

Full throttle through the night. D'you know what this baby can do? Push her to the limits. I'll go all the way with you...

And down by the sea and the spiky Pandanus tree, we drive. Watching the water and that orange glow to the north, beyond the mangroves.

You take me past the park where they hold the Spring Parade, and the Sea Scouts' den, and the house with the crazy cockleshell garden and gnomes through all the flower beds. You drive me out to the yacht club and down a secret road. It takes us right out along the harbor wall to the ships' entrance.

You pull up and hop out and the wind is strong here, beating the water into a black chop.

"How do you know about this place?"

"This is where all the guys from school take their girlfriends." A smile crosses your face.

"Oh, speaking from experience..."

"Yeah, that's it," you say, laughing, "Hey, you know my track record on that one."

"So you've taken me to some make-out point. Should we be expecting the drive-in crew to turn up in their sloppy jalopies?"

"Their what? No, I don't think so. I'd say we have this place to ourselves tonight."

A light dances in the distance. It lights up the side of the car and holds in your eyes. Seconds later there's a crunching of tires on gravel. Lights flicker, horns blast, and a procession of panel-beaten family vans and backfiring Falcons comes by. Engines are cut and headlights fade. Passengers tumble out like carnival clowns. A bottle makes the rounds.

"Hey, look who it is," someone calls, "We saw your car from the Esplanade."

"Hey, Toby. What's going on, mate?" you say, crossing to an open car door.

And all the girlfriends have dazzling eyes that dance when you aren't looking; and the boys tussle and tap you, jostling and joking. You are one of them, and yet you aren't, and for a moment I see how trapped you are.

"I have to be home soon," you tell me, when you break away for a moment. "Let me say good-bye and I'll drop you back."

But the boys have stopped laughing. They look grim and gray-faced in the moonlight, and they begin talking.

Exam block. Two weeks without school and no excuses for not seeing you. Two weeks of daytime movies, trips to the city and drives to the beach. When your mother leaves for work on Monday morning you call me and we plan a week of activities, with only minor breaks—for exams.

"Get ready," you say, "I'm coming to pick you up. We'll go swimming at my place, then down to Wynnum for a fish and chip lunch. What do you say?"

"So what does your mum do?" I say, as we're driving down Tingal Road.

"She's a supply teacher. Used to be a math teacher, but now she just goes and fills in for other teachers when they're sick."

"A math teacher? Yuck! I couldn't do that. I'm failing math as it is."

"Oh, she hasn't taught math since I was born. She only ever does supply. She used to come to our school all the time."

"Are you serious? Have you ever had her?"

"No, but my brother has once."

"Oh, really? How was she?"

"I think the words *psycho bitch* were used," you say, grinning.

Your house turns out to be on the other side of Wynnum completely. It's a one-story brick affair in a cul-de-sac off Manly Road, near the strawberry farm.

"Come on, I'll give you the grand tour," you say the moment we're inside, and you drag me through each of the rooms, starting at the pristine "TV room" and ending at yours.

I look through your CDs, your trophies, your books. You lie down on the bed and shut your eyes, but they're open the moment I sit down next to you. You're just watching me full in the face as I run my fingers down your side and across your waist.

"Shit!" you say, jumping to your feet suddenly. "Mum's back."

And you're out in the living room in under a second. I wander out to find you, confused and a little amused by all your carrying on. But as I walk past the garage, I hear the ticking of a cooling car and I know that this means trouble. Big trouble.

You're standing near the door, just bracing yourself. You look over at me sheepishly and point out the couch.

"What happened to your class?" you ask, the moment she enters.

"Oh, you're never gonna believe this. I got there and they didn't need me. This is after they woke me up at—Oh! Hello…" she says, stopping in her tracks.

You introduce me offhandedly and for a moment your mother just looks at me as if she's trying to work out where I fit in. Then she returns to her story. "I don't understand why they couldn't have called and canceled. I mean, why they had to wait till I got there—don't you have a BCT test to study for today?"

"No, I had my last test on Tuesday, remember? I'm on holidays."

"Whatever you say."

"We were just going for a swim."

She looks back at me. Her face is sun warmed, freckled, but the skin around her eyes is light. It makes her gaze seem more concentrated. I fidget on the couch.

You open the screen door and I follow you out over the warm cement to the edge of the pool. You kick off your thongs and strip down to your board shorts. Your body is still a surprise to me. I try not to look. Not with your mother so close.

You bend to the pool, test the water. I pull off my shirt and you're looking up at me, smiling.

"Hurry up then," you say, splashing water up at me. You rock forward, tighten and dip, elegantly breaking the water, disappearing.

I run and dive. The shock of cold water! Then bubbles...splashing. Splashes everywhere. Hands, water, and smiles everywhere. Then calm, panting...laughter... You, more beautiful than ever: half-covered, half-drowned, still smiling. Always smiling.

And then that sudden frown that makes me turn.

I can see her there too, watching us from the kitchen...making calculations...adding...deducting...

When I turn to face you again, the pool is empty.

I remember bobbing in the water alone and the sound of the pool gate shutting behind me as you left to look for your towel.

Aisle 7. Canned goods, soups, sauces, and condiments.

Woolies on a Wednesday. I'm hiding out by the tinned spaghetti. From here, there's a perfect view of your register. I'm a discerning shopper, who always reads the labels—always with one eye on the laser lad in 12 ITEMS OR LESS.

And here you are suddenly, swaggering up to me with that grin that I could take in for hours.

"Can I help you, sir?"

"Why, yes, actually. I was having a spot of trouble finding…"

And there we go flirting over tinned fruit…or candied popcorn…two-in-one shampoo…Shake 'n' Bake pancakes…two-minute noodles…

"My parents are going away this weekend," you say, "you should come and stay over."

"You serious?"

"Yeah, come over Friday night, have a swim, spend the night. What do you say? I'll pick you up from yours. Bring your togs—or don't. No one'll be home."

But when Friday came around there *was* someone home. Your brother.

"Sorry," you said, over the murmur of the running engine, "I forgot he'd be there. We could still go. He'll probably go to a party anyway."

"Or host one."

"True."

You turned off the engine and looked over to where I should have been sitting, then you turned back to me and smiled:

"I know where we can go."

How cold it was that night, by that windblown sea! We sat shoulder to shoulder on the hood of your car and tried to pick out the islands we knew.

There Moreton, there Mud, and Fisherman's, floodlit and green. Here Saint Helena, here Straddy, and tiny King.

"Can you see those northern lights?" I said. "What can they be? Some flame-nosed dragon? The orange glow of some unfinished dream?"

You scrambled down the rocks, to take a closer look. The

waves thrashed and surged. Salt spray clung to the air. I could taste it on your lips when you came back to me.

Eventually the wind forced us to retreat to the warmth of your car.

That night was tidal, and you washed over me like a rising sea, filling my straits and sea creases, wearing away barriers like yielded sandcastles.

You took me in you, washed and weathered me. There were depths and shallows. Unfathomed places.

And when the waters had subsided, and we'd surfaced a little different but unharmed, you turned to watch that all-night sunset, that midnight glowing beyond the borders of all we knew.

You let your head settle on mine. You let the wind blow with force enough to shake the moon from the sky. And you let me hold you as only I'd dreamt to, while we watched the black sea gray to blue...

The sun made no concessions for the sleep-deprived. It scowled through the windshield, searched us out in the backseat, until you squinted and sat up.

The tide was out. Around us, the sounds of popping mud and the measured tiptoeing of waders.

"I'm not ready to go home yet," I said.

"Let's just sit here awhile."

You pushed up, worked some sleep from your eyes, then wandered barefoot to the rocks to look out over the bay. No northern lights. No southern dark, no more. Just the coming of a bright day.

"Come on," you said, slipping back into the driver's seat, "I'll take you the long way home."

We drove past the harbor and the hill to the park with the big Bay Fig—children already deep in its dusty arms. You pulled into the little servo off the Esplanade, and while you filled the car I searched your glove box for clues. Evidence from a time before I knew you. Really knew you.

Then I heard your voice at the pump. Bright and cleansed. It was the voice of another you. The voice I'd heard you use with customers, that school captain voice.

"Man, I can't go anywhere without being seen," you said, dumping change into the ashtray.

"Who was it?"

"One of Mum's netball friends."

I glanced up to the rearview mirror, but we'd already pulled out of the drive.

"Did she see me?"

"I dunno," you said, and you smiled at me as though it didn't matter either way.

We drove in silence through the backstreets, passed the community center and the hospital. Then, when we reached the top of Manly Road, you leaned over and shut the glove box.

When we made it back to my street you took the corner a bit fast, pulled the handbrake on a bit hard, but the car still creaked and complained when I hopped out.

You opened your door and stepped onto the road. Your hair was messed and your eyes small and craving sleep.

"All right," you said, "good nigh—" and your voice slid into a hollow yawn.

You slumped over the roof of the car and the door rocked back, pulling you in close.

"Good night. Good night. Parting is such sweet sorrow..." I called.

You mumbled something dark, softened against the warm metal of the roof. Your fingers danced on without you, pulled back, pincers raised, like a menaced mud crab.

"By and by I go…" I called again.

"Mmm…buh-bye…" you murmured. A smile twinkled on your lips.

I left you standing there, cradled in the rusty arms of your car, on the border of sleep and waking. I was worried you might stay there all morning, biscuit-baking on the metal roof. You were still there when I reached the top of the hill.

"Where were you?" my mother asked as I made it through the front door. "We were worried. We nearly called the police."

I told her we'd gone to your place and I'd fallen asleep watching TV on your couch. She didn't buy it, but I didn't care, 'cause I'd felt the warmth of you against me in the first chill of day.

It seemed normal to want this. To want you—fully and freely, without hindrance or heartache. Mine forever and always, uncompromising…uncompromised.

For weeks after, my parents caged me with their questions. There was never a good enough lie to escape at nights.

During the school day, I thought only of you, and in the afternoons I rode the two extra stops on the train just so I could wander past your work. I became one of those teenagers that loiter in supermarket car parks, but I didn't sit smoking on any upturned milk crates. My over-the-counter addiction was far greater than any store-bought drug.

"When can I see you?" I said as I passed through your register one afternoon.

"I dunno… My parents are being really hard on me at the moment, say I need to knuckle down for my final exams."

"Yeah, I know. Same."

"Four ninety," you said, holding out your hand.

"I want to talk longer. I miss you."

"You need to buy more then," you said, grinning.

Our hands touched as I passed over the money.

"Call me," you said. "When I can escape, I'll come. You know I will."

But I couldn't escape now. Not even to make that call. I was distracted and it showed. Like any good addiction, the lack of you triggered symptoms of withdrawal. Or was that simply the burden of the secret?

One night when my parents pestered me about homework and assignments and the importance of not slackening off so close to the end, I exploded, yelling, "You wouldn't know what I did anyway!"

Mum looked at her plate. Dad threw up his hands as if to say, I don't know what to do with you anymore.

I bit my lip, excused myself from the table, went and did whatever I'd just said I'd done. Lied about.

I realized what I'd done and it scared me. I was laying down a challenge to them, urging them on, saying: Go on, find out. See if I care.

Not long after, my mother trapped me over a cup of coffee and asked me that question I didn't know how to answer.

"What did she say?" you asked me, when you called me later that night.

"She was okay… Said she'd suspected for a while."

"What about your dad?"

"He went away by himself for a while… Just sat outside and watched the water."

"Are you okay?"

Your voice was earnest. You wanted reassurance. I wasn't sure I could give it to you. I pressed the phone so hard to my ear that for a moment I thought I heard the ocean.

"I love you."

It was the most comforting thing I could say. My ear pressed to that shell, those captured waves breaking at the other end of the line.

"I love you too."

By the Bowls Club, where the wind rustles the palm leaves like so many birds taking flight, I found you waiting.

The moon so full there and the coast so clear—stretching before us like the night itself, so wide and so long.

"I wasn't sure you'd come," I said.

You walked straight into my arms and fell against my chest. And then, when you pulled free, I saw the expression on your face.

"My parents know," you said. "Mum went through my drawers. She found your books and your letters. My diary. They found everything. They know everything."

"What do we do?"

"I dunno. I didn't know what to do. She caught me at the door on my way in from work. She just started saying all these things. About you. About us, together. She wouldn't stop. Just kept going and going with all this stuff, till I thought I was gonna hit her."

I leaned in against you, put my arm around you for comfort, but you stayed tense, alert. I could feel you checking over my shoulder, scanning the horizon. And that's when you slipped— we both slipped. Fell into the deep end of some great dark pool. No life vests. Just oceans of guilt. Wave upon wave, crashing in all around us. And questions, so many questions... Questions enough to drown in.

What have we entered into? Almost without knowing. What risks are we running now? Were we better as we were? Just you and just me. No explanations. No declarations. We've made this love dangerous, by sharing it, haven't we?

We held each other and listened to the sea and the sound the palm fronds make in the breeze and I felt myself pulling your hand. Dragging you back to the wheel.

Come with me. Take me to the point, where the waves are dark and the sea seems endless against amber. Just once more, while we can. Away from the world and all its expectation.

Draw your arms around me, bottle me up and set me to sea. Years later, spilt on some sandy shore, I'll sit and tell you this story, the whole damn thing: how fast we lived and how warm the sky! How round the moon above us, bright as an eye! How I quoted Arnold in the dark hours as we watched the waves roll by...

And as we drove to the point, we were just two boys in a beat-up old car, like so many others, cruising the neighborhood for a laugh. Only one thing on our minds.

I don't think the difference showed from the outside, and I don't think it mattered, 'cause on the inside we knew exactly what it was.

That night, before you dropped me home, you pulled onto the gravel by Elanora Park and we looked out over the playing fields. We watched as the lights from the footy club went out solemnly and soon only the orange glow of the port warmed the sky.

"Maybe we should end this," you said. "I feel lost in all the lies."

"But we've spent too much time together... You're too much of a love to me."

"It's so hard," you said. "I want to be with you, but it's too much for them... Maybe in a couple of years... They just need time to get used to it."

"I understand," I said.

The sky looked so hot, like the air itself had caught fire. I could feel it warming at the corners of my eyes.

"I'm sorry," I said, blinking away the flames. "I'm sorry for all of this."

And then? Did I kiss you? Did I hold on for dear life—make that kiss last as long as I could? How did I let go so easily when it was over?

I opened the door and stepped onto the road. You just kept looking over at me, the whites of your eyes glinting in the darkness.

"I'll see you," you said. But there was no *soon*.

I nudged the door shut and stepped back. The engine snarled as you turned the ignition; gravel rumbled under your tires. It was too much noise for such a night and you waited till you'd reached the road before you hit your lights.

The park was one black mass, under an orange sky. I could see the bay lights beyond sparking and fading off the islands, throwing ricochets of color into the dark.

And I waited, until all that was left of you was the distant twinkling of your taillights along the Esplanade. Just two red pointers, marking out the way to some forgotten constellation in the cool, dark night.

A NOT-SO-STRAIGHT DUET

Natty Soltesz

1. *Bradley Gets Fucked*

Bradley went on AmateurFratDudez.com and looked at himself. His perfect, almost-naked body, pictured there for the world to see, was posed right next to the perfect, almost-naked body of his best friend Joe. The title of the video told the story in a nutshell: *Bradley Gets Fucked.*

He clicked through the still pictures. He looked good. Joe looked good. Their impossibly muscled bodies, the result of so many hours in the upper campus gym, showed off well.

He wondered if Joe had seen their page since it had gone up. They hadn't talked about it since the shoot, almost a month ago. Bradley was the experienced one, the star, having done several solo videos for the site before. When he'd been offered a thousand bucks to go all the way with another guy, the only one he could imagine doing it with was Joe.

He'd been surprised to realize the money felt like both a reason and an excuse.

Bradley gazed at an image of himself bent over, his plump asscheeks wrapped around Joe's big dick, a look of pained pleasure on his face. Had it all been acting? There was no denying that getting fucked had made him cum hard and fast—the proof was on video. Maybe he could rationalize by saying the Viagra made him do it, but truthfully, hadn't there been more to it? Was it just the newness of feeling something up his ass? Or the fact that that something had been Joe's cock?

Bradley rubbed his half-hard dick through his workout pants. Joe, on the screen, had his tongue in Bradley's ass. Bradley took off his pants, got on his bed, and threw his legs over his head. And without even thinking, in the absent and unafraid way we do secret things when we're alone, he wet the tips of his fingers in his mouth, brought them to his clean, slick asshole, and reminisced.

That Friday night, after the bars had closed, Joe drove the two of them back to Bradley's place. It was where they usually hung out, because Joe still lived in the frat house. Bradley had made good money doing videos, and had his own apartment off campus.

The silence in the car was edgy. They were alone, half-buzzed.

"So, have you checked out the site yet?" said Bradley. "They put up our video."

"No shit," Joe said, shooting Bradley a smile. "How do we look?"

"Pretty fucking good, I think."

"Man, that was so crazy."

"I know. But not too bad, right?"

"Yeah, it wasn't too bad." The light turned green. Joe shifted gears.

"So did you get, like, turned on at all?" Bradley asked.

"I don't know. I know it felt pretty good for me. You got a nice, tight ass." They both cracked up. "What did you think of it?"

"I really liked it," Bradley said, maybe wanting to shock Joe. "I don't know...having your dick up my ass sorta did something to me."

"Well, there must be a reason gay dudes like it, right?"

"Yeah, for real. You were, like, hitting a spot up there or something...."

They laughed again, and before any of it had time to sink in they were at the twenty-four-hour beer distributor, picking up a case as they did every Friday, almost out of habit.

The night was hot, and Bradley stripped to his underwear as soon as they got upstairs. The apartment was quiet, fraught with a strange tension. Bradley went into his bedroom, pulled up the site, and called Joe in. He leaned over Bradley's shoulder, and they looked at themselves on the website. Bradley could smell Joe's cologne.

"Crazy shit, huh?" Bradley said once they got to the end of the preview pictures. Joe sat on the bed.

"So you kind of liked it, huh?"

"Yeah," Bradley said, his hand idly dipping inside his underwear. Joe had a huge smile plastered on his face.

"I'd fuck your ass again," he said.

"I bet you would," Bradley countered. Joe just shrugged. Bradley felt his dick starting to get hard. "Actually, what felt the best was when you ate out my ass."

"You liked that, huh?" Joe said, standing up. His fat shaft strained against the front of his shorts. "I'd do that again, too."

"For real?"

"Yeah, man."

"You're out of your fuckin' mind."

"Who cares? We're both horny. Nobody's gonna know. We've done it before."

"Yeah, for a thousand bucks," Bradley said. He knew he was protesting too much. He couldn't stop himself.

"Get up," Joe said. "Get on the bed. I'll eat you out, dude." Bradley chuckled, but he could tell Joe was serious. So he shrugged, looked Joe in the eye challengingly, and pulled off his underwear. He had a perfect ass.

"It's clean, right?" Joe asked.

"Yeah, fucker. I took a shower before you picked me up." Bradley got on all fours on the bed, and presented his ass to his friend. He kept his eyes down as Joe got behind him, took Bradley's ass in his hands, and spread his cheeks open. His butthole squinched uncontrollably.

Bradley half expected Joe to slap his ass and say the joke was on him.

But Joe didn't hesitate. He sank his face right into Bradley's crack, his tongue going right for his bunghole. Bradley gasped, and his cock spasmed.

"Oh, man. Holy shit." Almost immediately he could feel that something was different from the last time. Joe was eating him out like a starving man. He licked and sucked Bradley's ass with enthusiasm, spearing his tongue straight inside, pressing the whole of his face until it was buried in butt. His tongue circled in and around Bradley's hairless, pink asshole.

There were no camera angles to worry about. No one was watching, nobody had to see. They could do whatever they wanted.

Bradley looked back. Joe was fondling his hard-on through his shorts. He thought about what he'd said earlier: *I kind of liked it. You hit a spot up there.* Had he revealed too much of himself?

They'd fucked on film with cool detachment. They'd done what they had to do, gotten off, gotten paid.

But Bradley knew his friend's reputation. He'd heard Joe boast that he could fuck all night. Now he was going to be on the receiving end. Joe was going to have his way with him. The thought was scary—and thrilling.

Joe took off his shirt and pulled off his jeans. His heavy, uncut dick flopped out from a thatch of trimmed pubes.

Bradley flipped onto his back and drew his legs up to his chest. He touched his hole and was surprised at how easily one of his fingers slid inside.

Joe laid his body atop his friend's. They crushed and ground their solid bodies together, Joe's slablike pecs and ripped abs sliding smoothly against Bradley's equally muscled torso. Joe held Bradley's legs up as he slid his fat peg back and forth against his hole.

He brought his face close to Bradley's, and for a moment Bradley thought they were going to kiss. He was relieved when Joe turned to suck on his neck. They had kissed in the video; that had been part of the deal. Nothing about it had felt right.

Joe stood up, his heavy, leaking dick hanging like a baby's arm from his body. He grabbed Bradley by the thighs and scooted him to the edge of the bed, licked his hand, smoothed the spit on the end of his prick, and lined it up with Bradley's soft anus. He slowly applied pressure until Bradley relaxed, and about an inch sank inside. Bradley gasped and held his breath.

"My lube's on the desk," he said.

"Condom?"

"In the drawer." Joe grabbed it, lubed up his dick and then Bradley's ass, slowly sinking his fat index finger inside. Bradley moaned, relaxed, let the finger in.

Joe got back into position, sank the head of his dick back in and, unable to resist the exquisite warmth and tightness of his friend's asshole, quickly horned the rest of his cock up Bradley's butt, balls-deep. Bradley looked at him with wide eyes. He wasn't in pain. What was he feeling?

There was no pretense this time, they were fucking to fuck, to get off, pure and simple. Joe pumped Bradley's ass slowly at first, finding a rhythm, and then going with it. When he'd fuck in all the way, his hips jammed tightly against Bradley's ass and thighs, Bradley would feel something come over him. It sent him outside of himself. He was stroking his still-rock-hard dick, but the pleasure wasn't entirely there. It was coming from the inside.

Joe fucked without thought, without mercy; he was a man with his dick in a warm hole, and Bradley knew how good that felt, and empathized. What pleased Joe pleased Bradley, and there was no reason to wonder, no reason to be anxious or concerned. They knew each other, they knew each other's bodies. They were both enjoying the fuck out of this.

"Fuck me man," Bradley uttered, and Joe obliged, sinking all of his nine inches into his best friend's beefy butt, feeling Bradley's asshole clench him tight.

Bradley looked into Joe's eyes. Joe was a good guy, but he was also kind of a lunkhead. To see him fuck, though, was to see him in his element. He worked his body fluidly, looking for all the world like a man who was born to fuck.

Bradley knew he was going to cum in spite of any efforts he made to hold back. "Fuck me man," he said again. "Are you close?"

"Yeah," Joe said, his hands grasping Bradley's legs, holding them in the air as he took his friend from above. "I can go at any time, bro."

"Cum with me, man. Cum in my ass." Bradley's hairless balls

scrunched up high in their sac. Joe banged and banged, sending it closer for Bradley each time. Bradley wasn't even stroking himself, and suddenly his cum was pumping, his load shooting out of his cock and landing on his sweaty stomach. Joe reached down to help his buddy pump it out, but it was too late and too sensitive, and Bradley knocked his hand away.

"Holy fuck. Holy fuck," Joe said, staring into Bradley's eyes. Bradley sensed the pressure building, and then he knew that Joe was letting go, grinding high and deep and shooting his cum into Bradley's ass; cumming inside, the way it was supposed to happen—not with the forced coldness of an obligatory cum shot. Joe let go of his legs and fell down onto Bradley's sweaty body, his dick still firmly planted in his rump.

So what was next? There were no cameras to stop rolling, no lights to shut off, no money to collect. Bradley breathed with his friend, pooled cum sticking them together. This had really happened. He ran his hand down his friend's broad back, and he wondered, if they were to fall asleep like this, would it be okay?

2. *The Morning After*

Sonny was sitting at the table, clutching a bottle of beer, when Chuck walked into the room. Their eyes met.

"Good morning," Chuck said. What else was there to say? As soon as he'd woken up, it had all come back to him. As far as he was concerned, there was no point in pretending it hadn't happened. He rubbed the sleep out of his eyes to avoid Sonny's glare.

Sonny bounced his leg, gulping more beer, never averting his stare. Chuck tensed. *How were they going to deal with this?* It was too much to think about. And he had a wicked hangover.

"Is there any beer left?" he asked. Sonny jerked his shaved head in the direction of the fridge. Chuck ambled over, scratching himself through his boxers. He hadn't bothered to get dressed. Sonny had put on his sweatpants.

He opened the beer and walked back over to Sonny.

"All I'm saying is…" Sonny's voice was low—the sound of a dog cornered and snarling. "…If you tell one fucking soul what happened last night, I will kill you. And I mean that."

"What?" Chuck said, holding the beer out to his side.

"You heard me."

"Dude, why the *fuck* would I tell anybody? You've got to be fucking kidding me."

"Just so you know. You breathe a word about this shit to anyone, and you're dead. And you know for a fact I'm not fucking around."

"Dude, would you just chill the fuck out? Seriously. You think I want my girlfriend to hear that shit? You think I'd want it to get back to anybody?"

Sonny stood up. Though shorter than Chuck's dark-haired, six-foot-two frame, Sonny was a tough little fucker—a fireplug of a dude with a chest full of tight muscles under smooth, tattooed skin.

He got in Chuck's face, his body loaded like a spring. Chuck, startled by his friend's aggressiveness, stepped back.

"We were drunk, dude. We were drunk, and shit got out of hand, *that's all*. Now you're all up in my face, for whatever fuckin' reason. What's your beef, dude? You wanna go?"

Sonny pushed Chuck's shoulder, sending Chuck reeling backward until he found his bearings and pushed back, hard. Sonny crashed to the floor, startled. Then he sprang up, like a tiger out of a cage.

He pounced on Chuck, sending a hard fist into his side. Chuck grabbed him around the waist and threw him to the ground. They rolled, struggling for control. Sonny got his hands around

Chuck's neck and squeezed. It took all of Chuck's strength to push and kick him away. He twisted out, flipping Sonny onto his back and holding him down by sitting on his thighs. Grabbing hold of Sonny's wrists, he pinned his arms to the floor above his head. Sonny writhed and squirmed. He was trapped.

"What do you want?" Chuck growled, as soft as a whisper. "What do you *want?*" Sonny stopped thrashing, catching his breath in great gasps. For a moment their bodies heaved, their eyes locked. That's when Chuck realized: Sonny was hard, his cock pressed like a diamond rod into Chuck's crotch.

Sonny started to struggle again, futilely; then he was writhing, hunching his body up against Chuck's. Chuck's cock engorged quickly, as though the blood and aggression were surging from his head and body right into his cock.

Sonny's eyes were searching and confused. Chuck yearned to do what they hadn't done the night before, and he went with it. Sonny met his mouth, hard, their teeth knocking together, drawing blood from Chuck's mouth. They kissed. Chuck was totally hard now, and he ground his erection into his friend, his tongue diving between Sonny's lips.

He sucked on Sonny's neck, keeping him pinned to the floor. Sonny thrust his hips, unabashedly humping against Chuck's body. Their tongues wrestled for position. Then Chuck released Sonny's arms, and Sonny made no attempt to roll away. He reached under Sonny's tight midsection, pulling their bodies even closer.

Their breathing was short, but the sex accelerated. Chuck worked his mouth down Sonny's body, sucking his chest and nipples, licking and biting his stomach. He pulled off Sonny's pants—his cock caught on the elastic and slapped right back against his stomach. Chuck nibbled around the soft skin of Sonny's pelvis, and when he got to his pert pink cock he didn't hesitate—he took it in his mouth, and sucked deep and tight. Perfect fit. Sonny whimpered.

Had they been viewing themselves in a rational state of mind, it would have been like viewing someone else, something from which they would have averted their eyes. Chuck slurped his buddy's cock like a Popsicle, and Sonny swept his hands through Chuck's hair, fighting back his orgasm.

Chuck ran his fingers under Sonny's balls. He was so smooth down there, sweaty from their struggle, and Chuck's fingers slid naturally toward Sonny's hard asshole. When his fingers made contact both knew that it was right. Sonny's whimpers became moans, and Chuck's cock got impossibly harder.

Chuck went down further, licking Sonny's taint. His flesh was so clean, so smooth—Chuck was barely aware of what area he was licking until his tongue made contact with the ring of muscle between Sonny's cheeks. It wasn't bad, so he dug in deep, working Sonny's hole with his tongue. It was as if his cock knew where it wanted to go, and his tongue was paving the way.

Sonny's asshole was soon wet with slobber. Chuck pressed a finger in and Sonny's butthole, hot and tight, took it like the mouth of a hungry baby. Chuck pumped his finger in and out while stroking Sonny, whose every muscle undulated as Chuck's hand reached it. He wrapped his arm around Sonny's shoulders and pulled him up. They kissed.

Sonny bent over and took Chuck's massive prick into his mouth. It was a blow job almost out of duty, with Sonny using more spit and slobber than necessary. Both knew where they really wanted Chuck's cock to be. All of this—lasting only minutes—was a precursor to the main event.

Chuck raised Sonny's legs into the air, lining up his wet cock. Sonny looked down, holding his breath. Keeping his cock steady with one hand, Chuck pressed forward. It took a minute, but then he was inside. Sonny winced at the pain at first, but then his ass let Chuck's cock in like a welcome friend. Chuck was balls-deep, and they were both where they wanted to be.

They were where they had been last night.

For Chuck, the night had seemed like a long continuation of the same dream. One minute they'd been doing shots in Sonny's bedroom, the cards long forgotten, the room beginning to spin. The next minute he was waking up in the dark, in Sonny's bed. He was fucking Sonny's ass, and it felt wonderful. Though he wasn't sure how he'd arrived there, he knew it was okay, because Sonny was panting under him. And Chuck had reached down and felt that Sonny was just as hard as he was.

So they'd fucked until they came, he in Sonny's ass and Sonny all over the sheets. Then they'd passed out a little, and later on they were fucking again. The second time lasted longer—but then maybe it had been several times that all merged together. At any rate, it seemed like they had fucked all night. Had Sonny ridden his friend's dick like a preteen girl on a prize pony? Had Chuck really opened his mouth to catch some of Sonny's jizz? Yes, yes, it seemed that they had.

The experience had been a bit murkier for Sonny. He wasn't sure what had set the events in motion, though he'd been vaguely aware of feeling his friend's hard cock pressed against him, and reaching down to feel it—but then he'd been very, very drunk. When Chuck had taken hold of him he'd just let go of everything and allowed him to take the lead. His head had gone elsewhere, and all he knew was the pleasure of the moment.

Then he'd woken up in the cold light of day and everything had come crashing down.

Chuck had Sonny's legs in the air and he was thrusting into him with no mercy. He slipped a strong finger between Sonny's lips and Sonny bit down, sucking it into his mouth as Chuck's thrusts got deeper and harder. Chuck instinctively knew that this was how his friend wanted it—rough and unforgiving.

They fucked in a silence punctuated only by deep, animalistic grunts each time Chuck drove it all the way home. Sonny's hole was tight like a wrapped-up rubber band; it felt like where Chuck's cock needed to be.

He flipped Sonny over and fucked him doggy style. Sonny looked back over his wide shoulders, down to his two mounds of butt that were stuffed with Chuck's cock. Chuck started stroking him. It wasn't going to be long.

Sonny arched up and Chuck held his torso close, sucking on his neck as he fucked into him.

"Gonna fuckin' cum," he whispered in Sonny's ear. At those words Sonny's cock jerked in his hand and started spraying cum, showering his chest and abs. Chuck lost it too, driving his monster prick deep inside and letting it loose, shooting cum all the way up his buddy's butt, holding still as he unloaded the first jet, then giving a sharp jab, then more cum, another jab, more cum, until he was empty.

He ran his hand up Sonny's torso, smoothing Sonny's cum into his skin like a lotion.

They fell onto the floor on their backs beside each other, gasping for breath. After a while, Sonny's breathing slowed. He was falling asleep. Chuck turned to his friend and held him, wrapping his arm around his chest. Sonny took hold of his hand and held it close to his heart, his ass cupped by Chuck's pelvis, their bodies pressed close for warmth and comfort.

The weariness of exertion began to overtake Chuck, too. Sonny was fully asleep now. They were holding each other on the hard floor. The refrigerator kicked on. Everything and nothing had changed.

FALLING

Simon Sheppard

$D_{ear You,}$

Of course I remember how we met, and so do you. After a decade together, though, there are some discrepancies between our two accounts. Actually, there always were. You swore that I butted into that queue to get into the movie sooner, but that's not true. I only did it because you were waiting there with someone I knew. Okay, he was a fuckbuddy of mine with a really big dick, but I only went up to you guys to say hi, and then the line started moving and I was just sort of swept inside. Is that a crime?

Oh, and you claim that I was after you from the first. Well, if I had been, wouldn't I have found some way to weasel myself into sitting with you guys for the film? But I dutifully let you two go sit alone, figuring it was some kind of date. Which you later told me it was. So "after you" would be an overstatement. "Intrigued," yeah, probably. Intrigued enough that I was happy when I ran into you again less than a week later. And you were

by yourself that time. Intrigued enough so that more than a decade after that movie (which turned out to be lousy, we both
agreed), here we are.

Funny how once-separate lives become entwined. It can be
so—yes, I'll use the word—beautiful. I know, I know, almost every time I get like this, you make one of those wry faces of yours.
David Mamet says, as you never tire of quoting, that "cheap
sentiment is enduring, and so is cheap scent." But maybe David
Mamet never woke up, walked into the kitchen, and had you
wave and smile that smile of yours at him before he went off to
write another play. No, I'm pretty sure he didn't.

And he didn't go with you on that Caribbean cruise last year,
either. "I'll hate cruising," you said—typically, after the nonre-
fundable final payment had been made—but you didn't. And it
turned out it was just as well we didn't opt for one of those all-
gay cruises, either. Our straight shipmates were just fine with us
slow-dancing together, or if they weren't, they wisely kept their
heterosexual mouths shut. And, hey, you managed to suck off
some married guy in the steam room. Twice. Which made for
some interesting times when you pointed him out by the pool,
he and his theoretically oblivious wife canoodling in the Jacuzzi
like newlyweds. But, hey, I don't judge. Much.

And the sex we had in that cramped little stateroom? It was
amazing. Like *we* were the ones who were newlyweds. You
hadn't fucked me in quite a while before then, but we were
both drunk on the cheap champagne the friendly cruise director kept pouring at the gathering for gay passengers. (The
"Friends of Dorothy" meeting—hah!) We tottered back to our
cabin, the rough seas not helping matters, and pretty soon I
was straddling you, your big old condom-clad cock inside me.
It was…well, far be it from me to get sentimental. But it was
amazing. You know it was. I bet even the cabin steward, dealing

with the stained sheets the next day, knew it was. Amazing.

That was, of course, just after I found out I had chronic hepatitis. I'd wanted to keep it a secret from you, till after the cruise was over, and somehow I managed to. You knew something was wrong, but I managed to bullshit my way through. While we were fucking, though, I thought *God, we're fucking like this is the last time we ever will.* Pretty meaningless, really, since anytime anybody does anything, it might be for the last time. But, yes, that evening in the stateroom, I did have sex like my life depended upon it. I bet we looked quite the sight when we went down to dinner. Like we glowed. And, hep C and all, I knew that life was sweet.

It was tough on you when I shared the news. But you came through like a trouper, seeing me through the treatment, trying to keep my spirits up when the fucking dreadful cocktail of drugs made me want to lie down and die. We made it through that, you and I, and the day my viral load test came back marked "undetectable," you said, "Let's go on another cruise," and I said, "Sure, but in the meantime, let's fuck like we were back onboard already."

And yeah, there were tears in your eyes, but I bet even David Mamet would have gotten moist.

Aw, shit, it's later than I thought. More later.

Love,

Me

Dear You,

It's one of those gray, rainy days that call for cuddling. But since you're not here, I'll spend some time remembering. For all the "be here now" stuff—and hey, I know that Truly Living in the Eternal Present is the only way to go, honest I do—memories are lovely, ain't they? Kind of especially when they're memories of *you.*

Our first year or so was the hardest, I guess. At least for me. You'd just broken up with Pablo, and were not, by your own admission, over it yet. Which meant that I would hear about him. Not a whole lot, but more than I wanted to, enough to make me wonder what you were thinking about when you got that faraway look in your eyes, enough to make me wonder if you were thinking of him while you were fucking me. Fortunately, we'd agreed from the first that whatever relationship we were going to have would be an open one, so when the strain of being The One Who Was Not Pablo became too much, I was able to go out and, almost guilt-free, get fucked elsewhere. But I never really told you—till now—how hurt and confused your bloody masochistic nostalgia sometimes made me feel. I mean, darling, it really got to be a drag. Really.

Now that I come to think of it, you really can be a putz sometimes. But I suppose I got my own back when I fell for Brian, huh? Jesus, what a fiasco *that* turned out to be…though it was fun while it lasted. I guess…

Okay, maybe it was less than fun, chasing after a manifestly unsuitable crush while you waited patiently at home. At least when you weren't trolling the bars or fucking your brains out with some hot stranger. But I digress, don't I? Brian…Jesus… Brian…

Oh, sweetie, it *is* so damn gray outside, the sort of day to cuddle under the duvet with you and kiss. Whenever I read something out of those tacky erotica anthologies you for some reason like to drag home, I'm always struck by how undervalued cuddling is. Kissing, too, for that matter—porn's always all about cock. But sometimes I think that cuddle-time is the sweetest part of the day. It's certainly what I miss most acutely just now.

Later: I've taken a break from writing, but I'm back. I've been thinking about you. Well, I always think about you, but

I've been thinking about the blog thing. You always were a lovably opinionated scold about politics, ever since I met you. But then your nephew got killed in Iraq, and you got angry, so angry. You started your blog more as therapy than anything else, just threw the words out there, not knowing if anyone would read them, and you were genuinely surprised when it took off, began receiving thousands of hits a day. I was always more reticent about speaking my mind than you, so I suppose you never knew how much I shared your delight the day you discovered that you'd been taken to task, by name, by some rightwing cocksucker at the *National Review Online*. Now I'm sorry I didn't bake you a cake or something to celebrate. If you were here right now, I'd give you a big, belated congratulatory hug.

But you're *not* here.

Love,
Me

Dear You,

The last few days have been rough. With you gone, it's been hard to care about anything. Haven't hit the gym, called in sick to work, dishes have piled up. You, neat freak that you are, would be appalled.

And I haven't been able to write you a letter, either. I'm only writing this now because, well, because I forced myself to.

I just went online to read some of your old blog entries. It's sort of hard, knowing you wrote that, yet not quite being able to reconcile all that righteous indignation with my memories of the sweet, insecure, often-depressed guy who shared my life. Wow, what a firebrand I fell in love with. Who knew?

Certainly not the straights at our dinner table on the cruise. Looking at the polite, well-dressed fellow tucking into his lobster tails, I bet they never suspected you'd written a piece excoriating monogamous married homos for "betraying the promise of early queer radicalism." And Jesus, you have no patience, no patience at all, for men who remain in the closet, not out of economic necessity or fear for their lives, but just because it's easier for them that way.

Oh, wow, why am I writing about politics, when all I want to do is kiss you, kiss you forever?

I miss you so much.

I'd better go do the—long overdue—dishes before I break down.

Again.

And then maybe I'll head over to Blockbuster and rent a David Mamet flick. *Glengarry Glen Ross,* say. Or *The Spanish Prisoner*—I always liked that one. He writes so well about scams. Being cheated. I won't rent *Hannibal,* though, regardless. There's a limit.

Love,
Me

Dear You,

The sun is out at last, and I feel, for no reason at all that I can discern, giddily happy. David Mamet, eat your heart out. And no, I never did make it to Blockbuster. I figured a story about being cheated was the last thing I needed to see just now.

Your father has sent me a letter. I just couldn't get myself to open it, though. I need at least a few hours of feeling great. Remembering your smile. All those little things that a couple builds up over the years—common experiences, catchphrases, sentences that one guy starts and the other finishes. But most of all, your smile. Even when I first saw you waiting on line for that long-ago movie, I bet that I noticed your smile. How could I not, when it's the very best smile in the whole wide world?

Oh, god, I sound like a schoolgirl with a crush, don't I? But you know me. If anybody does, ever has known me, you do. You know what a bitch I can be. Okay, maybe you don't know *everything*. That guy who posts on your blog all the time, the "dude411" one who always launches into straight-acting closet cases? And insults the President? Hey, that's me. At first, it started as a one-off experiment, but then it was fun to have a secret identity, a little concealed corner of my life. And don't tell me that you knew all along, because I really don't think you did till now.

Fuck, your smile.

I wonder what your dad wants. He never writes me unless there's bad news or a request. God, you were right. He's such an unhappy man. Can't deal with him just now, though. Have to stay happy, for your sake if nothing else. And I wouldn't want to start another huge pile of dirty dishes, ha ha.

Okay, enough of thinking about your father. Let me think of pleasant things, instead. Us in Mexico, you climbing up that pyramid, scrambling up toward me. Us in bed, fucking like rabbits. Us. No one who hasn't been part of an "us" can quite understand it, I don't think. I mean, I always, like the old song says, wanted somebody to love. Needed. But I didn't understand what it would really feel like. To have somebody. To love.

It feels great.

And sometimes it feels like it could rip my fucking heart out.

Love,
Me

Dear You,
How could you? I mean, how could you?
Love,
Me

Dear You,

So what, really, am I doing writing all these letters to you? It's not as though you don't already know everything I'm telling you—okay, except the part about writing postings to your blog—and this isn't a conversation. I wish I could give you something of real value, instead. It's starting to feel almost as though I'm writing these for some stranger to read.

And let's say for the sake of argument that somebody somewhere did read these letters, some stranger. What would they mean to him? Would he be able to read between the lines, see all the desperate, glorious delusion? Or would he, like Mamet, just hear the tinny sounds of sentimentality?

Oh, fuck, without you I feel all alone. Without you, what use are words?

Now *that* sounded mawkish, didn't it?

When all I want is to remind myself of how much I love you. To remember all the good times.

Oh, fuck. I should give this up, for the time being. I'm going to go watch "Entourage," I guess, then jump in a warm bath, smoke a joint, jack off, and get to bed.

Love,
Me

Dear You,

So pain is always inherent in love, huh? Especially great loves like ours? I know, I know…it's a truism, a cliché. But it's still and all kind of amazing that anyone takes the risk at all, considering.

Hey, I know you always like to hear about my weirdest tricks, so…

The other day I found this guy online, a bi with a great picture who wanted to get his dick sucked. Well, you know, that was an offer I couldn't refuse. So he shows up with his laptop and lays it down next to us on the bed, and there I am giving the guy the very best head I possibly can, and meanwhile he's fiddling with the mouse pad of his iBook, watching Quicktime clips of straight porn. Tits. Chicks with big boobs. Suck, suck, suck. The things I get myself into when you're not around, huh?

Oh, Jesus, I'm rambling. But I need you. I need you so much. Yes, it's only words, but words are all I have to…Christ, now I'm channeling the Bee Gees…

Okay, that's better. Just took a break, got myself a cup of coffee, wiped the tears from my eyes.

At this moment, I would give anything to see your smile, hear your voice, smell your smells. Anything.

The thing we started so long ago, waiting on line for that movie. It's been quite a thing, huh? Quite a thing. People started mistaking us for brothers, then twins. Even I couldn't tell where you left off and I began.

And then…

Nothing lasts forever.

Nothing lasts forever.

Nothing lasts forever.

Nothing lasts forever.

It's been so long, months now.

Fuck, I am so fucked up.

I will love you forever.

Love,

Me

Dear You,

I didn't sleep at all last night. Oddly, though, I'm not the least bit tired. Now dawn has come, as perfect as dawns get. I'm looking out the kitchen window, out at your favorite view.

The sky is a softening pink, the birds, twittering like crazy, can be heard through the half-open window, there's a delicate but definite promise in the air. Whether that promise will be fulfilled, or will be broken, as so many promises are, is still up for grabs. And—not to sound maudlin, which you hate, or at least say you do—for each and every one of us, every dawn can be the last. And yes, I wish you were here beside me. I do, I wish that most of all.

But no, I'm not the least bit sleepy. Still, maybe I'll go lie down. I have those pills.

No, don't worry, sweetie. I won't hurt myself. I know you always worry about that. But there was just that one time.

It's a beautiful day. A beautiful fucking day.

Love,

Me

Dear You,

Okay, maybe David Mamet was right, and yet—

THE BIKE PATH

T. Hitman

D o you want to go for a bike ride, down the path?"

He is standing with his spine pressed against the big wooden post at the center of our antique house, no shirt on, when he asks this. He moves his naked back up and down on the rough burl, scratching it the way bears do in the wild, against tree trunks. The image charms me. It also excites me.

I'd rather take a walk, I think. But I answer, "Sure."

Bradley-Stephen smiles. He hasn't shaved on his day off work and the prickle of his cheeks and neck lends his usually trim goatee and mustache, silvering around his mouth, a wild, intensely sexy look. Butterflies take flight in my stomach, scattered by lust. It's almost a decade since I first felt this way for him, but he still has the power to freeze me with a stare, melt my insides with his smile.

Yes, I'd prefer a slow, effortless walk on this sunny, lazy late summer afternoon. But I give in to Bradley-Stephen's suggestion, because that's the key to a successful relationship, which ours is by every indication. A little compromise goes a long way. Nearly ten years, so far. And if we keep feeling the way we do about each other, there will be ten more, and ten after that.

As I've since learned, it doesn't hurt to have at least a few common interests with your partner when you enter into a monogamous relationship. I can recite, chapter and verse, the minutia from even the most obscure of films. Bradley-Stephen knows TV. He's football, a game that's all brute strength and force. Me, I'm summer baseball, lazy and precise. Bradley-Stephen likes to knock back a cold beer with dinner a few times a week, but I haven't touched a drop of alcohol since yarking my guts out twelve years ago at a freshmen college booze-fest. Bradley-Stephen spends his days swinging a hammer and slapping paint onto walls with a brush. Me, I sit my ass in an office chair and stroke keys for a paycheck. He's naturally athletic, whereas if I don't make the effort, the pounds creep up on me and get comfortable hibernating around my midsection.

We're not one of those cookie-cutter gay couples who exchange clothes and hook up to double the size of their wardrobe. We don't share a lot of the same passions. But we do enjoy wandering the paths that cut through the conservation woods behind the house we bought a few years ago, and from the moment we met, we haven't been able to keep our hands off of one another.

I love Bradley-Stephen, and he loves me. Great sex...yes, we do share that common interest.

Deering, the small, rural town where Bradley-Stephen painstakingly restored our formerly falling-down antique cottage on three pine-studded acres, boasts a great bike path. It winds through the downtown, cuts through the woods, and continues through a vast farmer's meadow, where its course gets mowed by herds of rare heritage goats and dairy cows. Couples need to do fun things together other than sex, and that bike path has provided plenty of opportunities for us to bond. And more than once, we've had sex there, too.

We bike away from the house, down Blueberry Hill Road to Bayberry, where the signs point us toward the woods. If we were walking like I'd wanted, we could have held hands, crossed through the brambles, and intersected the path from directly behind our property. This route, however, is bumpier, faster, and requires more effort. Bradley-Stephen shifts gears and glides onto the dirt trail. I feel like I'm pedaling flat, square wheels while trying to keep up with him. My balls ache as the treads pass from smooth, paved sidewalk to uneven dirt. Sweat drips down my forehead, then pours, stinging at my eyes, soaking my pits and crotch. Like all couples, Bradley-Stephen and I argue. Usually, it's over stupid little things, like when he leaves the toilet seat up or forgets to cap the toothpaste. Or when he takes me for a bike ride and taunts me from twenty feet ahead.

"How's the weather back there?"

I sense we're about to have one of those stupid arguments. I'm ready to shout at him to slow the fuck down, to let me catch up…it's not a race. But then, as if reading my thoughts, Bradley-Stephen slows his pedaling. He tips his head in my direction and shoots me a devilish smile. Whatever anger I briefly felt evaporates. There's mischief in that smile; he's so damn cute, I wonder how I ever could have lost my cool over something so ridiculous. Cute, and so fuckin' sexy, the desire for him that I experienced back at the house reignites. In between navigating the way ahead, I study his magnificent body. The way his bare legs shimmer in the light, the sun embossing his naked skin, a bead of sweat catching in the hair along one calf…heavenly distraction.

I can't see Bradley-Stephen's warm brown eyes through his sunglasses, but I feel them wandering over my body. There's a good chance they're mentally undressing me; that goofy, lust-filled smile on his handsome face betrays what he's thinking. Bradley-Stephen is about to turn thirty-five, but often, like most guys, he still acts like a kid.

I smile back at the sight of him, perched atop his ten-speed, tall and lean, wearing his baseball cap and his shades, his khaki cutoff shorts and the ratty T-shirt bearing the name of some town in New Jersey he hasn't been back to in years, the tops of his bright white socks sticking above his paint-splattered sneakers. He takes my breath away.

The cathedral of pines thins, then opens on the long stretches of meadow. The air is bewitchingly sweet with the perfume of mowed hay and late summer wildflowers. There's even a trace of Bradley-Stephen's scent to be detected, sweeping up to embrace me on the breeze. The bike path continues on for another half mile through the field. More trees loom on the horizon. From there, the trail swings back into a neighborhood on the north side of Deering.

Bradley-Stephen, glistening with sweat, pumps the brakes. His bike slows, drops back until we are even, and suddenly that mischievous grin is neck-and-neck with me.

"Hey," he growls, all cocky.

I suppress a smile. "Hey, yourself."

"Come here often?"

"Only when my husband drags me out here against my will," I fire back, not missing a beat.

"He must be a smart guy if he's marked a piece of ass as hot as you as his own personal property."

I sigh out a laugh at his statement, but my insides catch fire as I realize I'm pushing an erection against my bike's seat. I understand Bradley-Stephen well enough to finish his sentences, to anticipate his moves, his needs, so I know when he's horny and wants to fuck. *Finally.* My lust for him is about to be satisfied.

Bradley-Stephen comes to a complete stop. I hit the brakes, coast to a halt several yards ahead of him, and turn back to see that grin, those hidden eyes, that mouth. The strength departs my aching legs.

"What?" I ask, unable to adequately catch my breath. I already know *what.*

"Come here," he growls, kicking his leg over his ten-speed's ball-buster bar. He tips his chin toward a patch of tall grass behind us.

"Here? Now?"

"Oh, yeah…"

Bradley-Stephen leads the way, walking his bike through the timothy grass, wild buttercups, and the lazy black-eyed Susan flowers. His steps kick up that fragrant country-summer smell. Suddenly, my insides feel twenty years younger, imprisoned in the shell of a thirty-year-old man. Bradley-Stephen dumps his bike onto its side. I pursue and let mine fall, too. Then we join the bikes on the ground, creating a private, secret crop circle, safe from prying eyes.

Bradley-Stephen pulls me into a tight, sweaty embrace. The full press of his lips crushing over mine removes any doubt as to where this is leading. I'm so ready to go there with him, I no longer worry about garter snakes slithering through the grass, or that hikers are going to hear our grunts and groans and discover two men fucking just off the bike path. There is only the taste of his mouth, that clean trace of mint from toothpaste, the salt of his sweat, and the rough scrape of his goatee as his lips consume mine.

The scent of Bradley-Stephen's sweat fills my desperate

breaths. I place a hand against his chest and trace the contour of familiar territory through the damp, worn cotton of his T-shirt. From there, my fingers walk lower. The fur-lined tautness of his abdomen scrapes beneath my fingertips as they travel down the region of exposed flesh between the bottom of his shirt and the top of his shorts. I feel the button and the metal teeth of the zipper that separate me from his cock. I cup his thickness. Bradley-Stephen humps my fingers. From the corner of my eye, I steal a glance and see that he is already leaking pre-come. A circle of wetness stains his tented crotch.

An appeased growl sounds from deep in Bradley-Stephen's chest. His kisses shorten into gentle bites. It's my cue to move lower. Shifting position inside the little crop circle we have flattened into the meadow, I place my chin on the exposed patch of muscle just above Bradley-Stephen's groin. He reclines, stretching out with his arms crossed behind his head. It's the same position he and I have stared up at the stars from, back at our little homestead. I glance up to see he has popped a blade of timothy grass into his mouth and, while working to free his thickness, snort out a laugh.

"What's so funny?" he grumbles, that cocky grin still planted on his mouth.

"You. You're such a guy," I answer.

"Shut up and suck my dick, bitch," he says straight-faced, holding back the laughter. If we were home in bed, he'd probably have a beer in one hand and the remote in the other.

"I love you, you bonehead," I snicker, undoing his shorts.

"I love you, too, babe…"

I open his shorts. Bradley-Stephen is wearing gray boxer-briefs beneath, and they're musty with his sweat. I ease everything down to his knees. His cock is toughened to such stiffness that it snaps out and strikes his stomach with an audible pop.

His balls glisten in the late afternoon sunlight. Bradley-Stephen's raw, primal scent possesses me.

I toy with his balls, tugging on their loose sac. Bradley-Stephen moans his approval—as I know so well, he loves when I give attention to that part of his physique. The meadow sings with a counterpoint of chirring crickets. Somewhere in the distant trees, a mourning dove sings its familiar elegy. I lean down and brush my tongue along his length, tasting salt, sweat, and pre-come. Bradley-Stephen unknots his fingers. One hand lovingly cups the back of my skull, urging me to continue with gentle pressure. I take the straining helmet of his cock's head between my lips and slowly nurse down his first few inches. From there, I suck my way steadily deeper, stopping only when the coarse thatch of his pubic hair tickles my nose.

After so long together, owing to countless occasions in bed, I've learned how to adequately handle my husband's thickness. I rarely gag on his dick anymore, unless it's intentional, which I sometimes do because it excites him. Over the years, I've also learned that it's good to mix things up a bit to keep the sex fresh; with only the sun sinking toward the horizon to mark the passing of time, I alternate between teasing licks and hard sucks, and whenever Bradley-Stephen edges toward climax, I release him completely and only service his balls to prolong his pleasure.

At one point, I worry that his grunts will give us away. But there are no other visitors on the bike path today. It's just us, the crickets, the birds, and heritage breed dairy cows grazing somewhere far away.

I'm drunk on his taste, high on his scent. My cock, burning in my shorts, begs for release. Bradley-Stephen senses this, in that way couples who share a great connection are able to. Without asking, he begins to massage my ass through my shorts. The gentle ever-widening concentric circles intensify. Eventually, he tugs me toward him, away from his balls. Seconds later, I am on my back and Bradley-Stephen is pulling off my clothes.

Warm summer air gusts over me, followed by wet kisses that move steadily lower. A breath teases the sensitive flesh of my most private place. A feral grunt and a lick invade my asshole. Fighting the urge to shudder, I grab my legs behind my knees and pull them up, allowing him easier access to the prize he seeks. My husband has always been an ass man; by the time he stops licking me out, the sun has fallen noticeably lower, bathing the meadow in the last of its light, and my fuck-hole drips with his spit.

"*Yes*," I beg, after he briefly breaks our connection.

Bradley-Stephen moves into position on top of me. He lowers, again crushing our mouths together. I taste myself on his lips just as the pressure of his cock's head presses against the opening to my core. I seize in place beneath him when a jolt of icy-hotness tickles my insides. The mild pain at being invaded by my husband's length passes, turning to pleasure. We are linked now. Yin and yang. His hardness fitting perfectly into my softness. I encircle Bradley-Stephen's shoulders and hold on to him, pulling him even closer. The sun's waning light casts an aura around his face. The image of his magnificence overwhelms me.

"Fuck me," I moan.

Bradley-Stephen rocks forward, burying his cock deeper. The world temporarily shifts out of focus as a wave of pins and needles wracks me from ears to toes. He pulls partway out, then shoves in again, settling into his rhythm. My legs join my arms, wrapping themselves around him. I barely remember coming, just that at some untimed point in our lovemaking, Bradley-Stephen rubs that internal trigger spot beyond my ability to hold back another second. In doing so, I tease him into climaxing, too.

He collapses on top of me, and as has always been the case

since the first time we made love untold thousands of fucks behind us, he lowers back down between my legs and savors his
own taste.

I keep thinking, as the swirl of his tongue cyclones around
my asshole, making me levitate above the ground, how every
time we make love is like the first. After ten years of this, you'd
expect some of the fire to go out. It's only natural, because that's
what happens with couples over time. But it hasn't for us, not
yet. When Bradley-Stephen crawls back up, putting us face-to-
face on a carpet of flattened meadow, I cup his cheek. My expression, reflecting in his sunglasses, speaks volumes.

"You're the best," I whisper.

"No, you are."

"I wouldn't trade this for anything."

"You'd better not."

He fidgets back into his pants.

"It's getting late. Think you've got enough energy to make it
home?"

"I hope so," I grunt, pulling on my shorts. A stray blade of
timothy grass teases one of my buttcheeks.

"We don't have to ride the bikes," he says, standing and extending his hand. I take it, and Bradley-Stephen pulls me back to
my feet. "We can walk them back."

Give and take. Him and me.

"I'd like that," I say. And with twilight approaching, we start
down the bike path, headed for home.

THE COUNTRY HOUSE

Jameson Currier

Arnie always graciously warned his guests about what to expect at the country house: slamming doors, crashing plates, flickering lamps, the dogs out of control, even a spike in their own temperaments. "Mitch and I have been fighting more and more since we bought this house," he would add after he had extended an invitation to his friends to spend a weekend with them in their haunted country house. "I think our ghosts get a kick out of seeing us irritated with each other."

After five blissful years of living together in a tiny cramped studio in Greenwich Village, Arnie and Mitch found the large, rustic rooms of their weekend retreat both liberating and aggravating. Arnie, who fell in love immediately with the giant kitchen and new appliances, wanted to cheaply furnish the other rooms, but Mitch was headstrong about scouring the local flea markets and estate auctions for deals and had soon developed a taste for overpriced broken furniture.

"The drawers won't open," Arnie complained about an oak

hutch Mitch had found at a garage sale and brought back to the country house. "And the legs wobble."

"It's art deco," Mitch pointed out. "Look at the carving on it."

"And the shelves are missing. You got pinched on this one."

"I can get someone to fix the leg and put in a new shelf."

"And it'll end up costing more than it's worth. We should've bought something new."

"You can't buy a new antique."

"If it was new, you could have gotten a discount," Arnie complained, "not a four-hundred percent markup. What a waste of money, if you ask me."

"No one's asking you," Mitch answered. "Which is why I bought it."

Mitch and Arnie's country house is a ninety-minute drive from Manhattan, not far from the Delaware River and the canal and the quaint village shops of New Hope and Lambertville. Originally a small two-room stone cottage built in 1823, it was expanded in 1871 with a second floor and renovated and enlarged with a new wing a century later in 1983 by a well-known interior designer and his significant other. The property is outlined by the low-rise stone walls made from clearing the land for crops, and branches of the gnarly-trunked oak and maple trees shade the house in the summer and blacken in the winter months. A stone path, blistered by roots, leads from the road right up to the kitchen door. Inside, in the kitchen, is an enormous working hearth where the meals were cooked in the original house, along with the modern-day upgrades of a double-door Sub-Zero refrigerator, granite countertops, two ovens, and a six-burner grill. Upstairs, the master bedroom has a cathedral ceiling and a hot tub in the bathroom. Neither Arnie nor Mitch were any good at husbandry—carpentry, gardening, plumbing—and luckily all that was necessary before they moved in was to have the rooms painted and central air-conditioning installed, a process Arnie was insistent on and that meant sawing through the old floorboards and plastered ceilings of the house to install the vents, which had probably dislodged and disturbed the already restless resident spirits.

"Money well spent," Arnie confided in me one weekend when I was a guest at their house. "Or the humidity would have done us all in." I have known Arnie since our college days, long before we both reached our late thirties and he settled down into this high-maintenance relationship. Arnie loved to tease me with the details about why he felt he might soon be back on the market for a new lover: Mitch's overanalysis of every conversation, Mitch's dysfunctional home purchases, Mitch's ill-mannered table habits. And on and on. Arnie also confessed to me that he and Mitch had purchased the house with a significantly low bid—it had been on the market for more than a year after a series of married couples had bought and then sold the property after they had been unable to abide living with the cranky poltergeists.

"If I can live with Arnie, I can live with any sort of irritable ghost," Mitch would joke with their guests when they were entertained in the dining room with an elaborate three-course dinner by candlelight that Arnie had spent a day preparing. "You don't have to guess which one is easier."

This sort of banter always seemed to amuse their weekend visitors—usually other dramatic couples from the city: a gray-haired film director and the young actor-boyfriend he had rescued from hustling, the hefty lesbian couple who ran a pet-grooming salon in Chelsea, the anorexic European fashion magazine editor and her chain-smoking photographer-husband from Greece. During a weekend in the country, Arnie's seething resentment never failed to bubble to the surface. "I spend my entire time cleaning and cooking, while Mitch shops for old paintings and broken furniture," Arnie would pout, and rattle his dishes and pots through the warm water in the sink, since he had neglected to notice that his new state-of-the-art kitchen did not have a dishwasher and he had not a clue of how one could be installed. "It's an ideal arrangement for *him*."

Sometimes their argument would escalate—Mitch might criticize that the pot roast was too dry or that the lemon-apple tart was store bought; Arnie might announce how much money Mitch had been fleeced for on a seventy-year-old cracked cookie jar in the shape of a clown's face—and if a second bottle of wine had been opened the conversation could turn nasty and wounding, depending on the familiarity of the guests, the heat of the weather, or the difficulty of the recipes. Sometimes the dinner would be interrupted to clean up an accident created by one of the two hyperactive cocker spaniels that the couple had adopted in an effort to seem more like country squires—a swift swipe of a chicken bone from a guest's plate that could send it crashing off the table or a puddle of piss shot onto the wooden floor intended to garner their masters' attention (and hopefully deflect all the rising bad tempers). One weekend when I was there with my new boyfriend Scott there was a threat by one lover with a carving knife that ended in the other lover performing a headlock on him. The sudden and sheepish apology by both men to all in attendance occurred over after-dinner drinks poured from an expensive (and fractured) crystal decanter Mitch had found at an estate auction.

But much of the conversation during the couple's elegant inedible feasts would be spent on the ghosts of their country house, particularly if a guest had heard one of the phantoms slamming a door upstairs or tapping noisily at the window.

Arnie was rather fond of the door-slammer, in fact, except on those occasions when he wanted to take an afternoon nap. "Lucy—Lucinda was her real name—was the wife of the original builder of the house," he would explain, usually after Mitch had cut him to the quick with a wicked remark about a filmy fingerprint on a wineglass or a too-heavy hand with the garlic in a recipe. "Overworked and underappreciated. No wonder she just dropped dead one day. A little thank-you now and then always does her good."

Arnie liked to proudly explain that he thought himself particularly receptive to vibrations from the realm of the supernatural and Mitch loved to point out to their guests the hot spots of paranormal activity within the house, or, rather, the locations of strange, chilly draughts and severe drops in temperature. "Emma's bedroom, upstairs, at the far end of the house," he would usually begin his list. "There's a cold spot at the foot of the bed where she must have died. The dogs won't even go near it—they yelp as if someone has just stepped on their paws."

Emma was Lucy's daughter-in-law and believed to be the true source of any vicious disturbance in the house. "One morning I was standing at the top of the stairs and felt something push me," Mitch might tell the lesbian groomers or the European editor. "It was deliberate, like I was expected to lose my balance and fall and hurt myself. I could feel the anger in the air. It was as if something had conjured up all of Arnie's bitterness and I had stepped right inside it."

"Pity she didn't succeed," Arnie added.

No one had ever actually *seen* any of the ghosts at the country house, at least not during Arnie and Mitch's tenure, only heard them or felt them in the dark of the evening hours, which usually meant their weekend guests would greet one or both of their hosts the following morning with an odd source of their insomnia, an anecdote of sensing someone at the foot of the bed, the creaking sound inside the armoire, an eerie light going on and off in the hallway. As for myself, I never seemed to be any kind of spiritual magnet and have generally reached a deep and unencumbered slumber on my visits to their country house, particularly since I am out of the city and away from the noisy traffic beneath the window of my third-floor apartment on Ninth Avenue. One guest, however, Cheryl, an overweight and middle-aged out-of-work actress, said she sensed something strange in the guest bathroom one night, where there had never been a spirit presence detected before. "I felt as if someone were looking at me when I got out of the shower," she explained in a dramatic fluster of over-the-shoulder gestures. "I felt so vulnerable and exposed, like something was going to happen."

Mitch told Cheryl she had been watching too many teen slasher movies, but over an elaborately concocted cup of vanilla roast coffee served in a disfigured and chipped set of ceramic cow mugs that Mitch had found in a thrift shop in Buckingham, Arnie commiserated with Cheryl that perhaps it was because the ghost recognized her from the low-budget insurance-fraud commercial she had filmed over a decade before. Later, in private, Arnie told me that perhaps Cheryl had only *wished* someone were looking at her. "She's desperate for attention," Arnie said. "She hasn't been on a date for over a year and can't seem to get a callback audition."

Though Arnie and Mitch have never seen any of their ghosts, they have never regarded them with frivolity or contempt, especially since the quarrelsome couple prided themselves on being progressive, inclusive, and multicultural (even when they are at odds). Mitch, a psychiatrist, liked to think of their ghosts as part of their extended family, more welcome in his home than his demanding parents, needy siblings, and pampered nephews and nieces. Arnie, a corporate travel planner, is the more compassionate one, always trying to find a reason for the noise or the cold air, hoping that if he helps change the course of the haunting he might also alleviate any eternal pain; lighting a stick of incense to change the mood, for instance, or leaving open a book of poems or family photographs to soothe the restless soul.

"Emma likes all my divas," Arnie might explain to the theater director and his ex-hustler boyfriend about his selection of background music during dinner. "Show tunes. Opera. Madonna."

"But she goes wild when two men sing together," Mitch would add. "Duets. Chorus boys. Something always goes flying to the floor."

"We've been wondering if she was some kind of feminist or suffragette, but that is clearly anachronistic," Arnie said. "More likely she was abused. Put upon. Like many in this house are *still* treated."

But there is one haunting that the couple deliberately warn their weekend company to steer clear of at all costs—the linked spirits of two soldiers who fought in and survived the Civil War only to meet their grisly end in the stone cottage. The bodies of the two young men appear only at daybreak by the giant hearth in the kitchen, or so goes the legend, and a curse falls on those who witness them. "Never find yourself alone in the kitchen when the sun comes up," the real estate agent who sold Arnie and Mitch the property told the new homeowners. The sight of these two ghosts was a bad luck omen and the last straw that had driven all the married couples away. "A very unhappy ending," the agent whispered to Mitch. "And a bloody mess you wouldn't want to clean up," she told Arnie.

Peter Altemus was the son of the original builder of the stone cottage, Robert Altemus, who had built a new and larger house when his son became a teenager. By the time he was twenty Peter was broad-shouldered and clean-shaven, dark and sullenly handsome, and had the strength of one of the horses he used to plow the upper pasture in the spring. When Peter married Emma Frey, a woman from Philadelphia, the young couple moved into the stone cottage. In the years before and during the Civil War, Robert Altemus was part of the underground railroad movement, shepherding slaves northward by night to their hopeful freedom elsewhere. Peter had sat out the first months of the Civil War—there were the crops to attend to and a colicky but pretty new baby girl, Sarah Ann, to take care of. The young couple were used to seeing figures coming and going from the barn they shared with Peter's parents—Robert's hired hands, the escaping slaves, a wandering Union soldier—but it had never aggravated the women as long as the men were there to keep order. In 1862, Peter joined the Philadelphia regiment and left his young wife and sickly daughter in the care of his aging parents in the larger house, leaving the stone cottage empty and abandoned. In the spring of 1863, Robert Altemus was shot and killed while attempting to prevent a Union officer from taking one of his horses from his barn and Emma had written her husband with the news, begging him to return to the farm. That fall, Peter Altemus was captured and later transferred to the Confederate prison camp in Andersonville in 1864. In the last days of the war, Peter and Will Ogden, the Confederate officer who protected him at the camp and became his close buddy, left the prison and made their way on foot back to Peter's home in Bucks County, Pennsylvania.

At dusk one day Emma had seen the two men from the upper window of the larger house, approaching about a mile away on the main post road. She did not recognize her husband, his gentleman's posture changed by a broken foot and a bullet-wound through his shoulder, and thought instead that he was just another of a number of aggressive strangers the women had had to chase off the land. She saw them headed in the direction of the barn and the stone cottage and decided to let them spend the night, knowing that in the morning she might be faced with a difficult confrontation if they still remained on the property.

Before daylight the next morning, Emma arrived at the barn with her father-in-law's rifle, found no one there, and fed their last horse, a lame mare named Molly. The war and hard work had streaked Emma's brown hair with gray wisps that she was forever pushing away from her forehead with the back of her hand. It was daybreak when she approached the front door of the stone cottage. She found the two men in the front room, asleep by the hearth atop a pile of straw and a rubber coat, their arms and bodies entwined like lovers. She had only noticed the Confederate insignia on the discarded jacket when the first of the two men stirred, saw her standing by the door and reached for a knife he kept tucked in his belt. Emma Altemus shot Will Ogden in the heart before he was fully standing. She did not recognize her husband—he was slimmer and gaunt, his hair thinning and his face covered by a scraggly beard. She shot him as he was opening his eyes from sleep, awakened by the blast that had killed his mate.

Emma did not know what she had done until minutes later when, searching through jackets and pockets, she discovered a letter she had written her husband more than a year before. She looked at his name on the envelope, studied her own handwriting as if it were in a foreign language, then fell to her knees and began to cry.

The plan came to her about an hour later, as the dark red blood traveled along the floor to the place where she had collapsed. She dragged the bodies to the barn, burying the two men in a hole she spent several hours digging. She burned their uniforms and clothing in the hearth, which created a great and unnatural stench for most of the day. A slow, northeasterly wind prevented the odor from reaching the new house and her mother-in-law's notice, and Emma burned her own bloody clothing to hide any trace of the crime. No soldiers had ever been in the stone cottage, she decided. She would tell nothing to her mother-in-law. Her husband had died in the war, in prison, a Confederate retaliation for the Union victory, not from the trigger of a gun held by his own nervous wife.

All this had been recounted in a letter Emma Altemus had left for her daughter when she died in 1914. Emma had moved back into the stone cottage almost immediately after the murders; the felony had never been discovered, and when she remarried years later, her new husband added the second floor to the stone cottage. The larger Altemus house had been sold decades before Emma's death when Emma's mother-in-law Lucinda had died. By the time of her mother's death, Sarah Ann had married a printer in Easton and had had four children, and she had been too disturbed by her mother's news to have the barn floor excavated and the bodies located and properly buried. When no immediate buyer could be found for her mother's stone cottage, it lay abandoned until after the Second World War, when Sarah Ann's grandson began renting the property to an artist and his companion. From there the hauntings began, or, rather, began to be recorded. In his diary, the artist, Michael Franz, wrote of slamming doors and tapping sounds throughout the cottage. One morning, at daybreak, he smelled a strange odor in the kitchen and witnessed the bloody corpses of the two men on the floor beside the hearth. He fell ill later that same day, dying of pneumonia a month later.

During the next thirty years the legend of dual ghosts was widely publicized, primarily due to the posthumous renown of the artist and a big-ticket auction that included his Pennsylvania paintings and diaries. In the following years, however, the appearances of the ghosts of Peter Altemus and Will Ogden were sporadic and infrequent, though they were always preceded by a strange burning stench and witnessed at daybreak, always in the same spot beside the large hearth in the kitchen; their embracing last moments became entwined with mysterious or suspicious meanings, particularly since Michael Franz had referred to them in his diaries as "the tragic lovers of years past." And calamity, misery, tragedy, or just an endless run of bad luck seemed to haunt any living soul who saw them. Reese Tanner, the interior designer, who had the misfortune to see them in 1983 in the middle of his expansion of the stone cottage into a two-story country retreat, fared particularly badly. He saw them at sunrise, pooling in their own blood. He went upstairs to where his partner, David, was sleeping, roused him, and said he had just seen the two ghosts.

Afterward, Reese and David had only experienced some minor handicaps with the expansion of the house—a contractor who deserted them, a foundation that cracked and had to be repoured, windows built to the wrong size and then installed upside down. Reese was a handsome and persuasive man, however, thirty-eight and well built, and he often chose workmen who also liked to party after hours, particularly if David had remained in the city or was tied up with supervising another design job. One morning, about four months after his observance of the soldiers by the hearth, Reese noticed a reddish patch of skin by his collarbone, about as big as a one-carat diamond.

Other lesions appeared quickly thereafter, on his thighs, his arms, his chin, his nose. In the final stages of the disease, he lost his eyesight and never saw the completion of the renovations of the country house, which David reluctantly finished on his own. David never spent another night in the house after Reese's death, however, selling the property to the first married couple who would take it off his hands.

And as for the fate of the more recent slew of married owners, the details I heard were secretive and limited, but among the words Arnie and Mitch whispered to me one night at the dinner table were *miscarriage, adultery,* and *cancer.*

When my boyfriend Scott first heard the tales of the ghosts of Arnie and Mitch's country house he disbelieved my theory that the two soldiers in the Civil War might have been murdered and buried by a jealous Emma Altemus. "I don't doubt that the two soldiers may have had some kind of sexual intimacy with each other—or certainly some kind of intimate bond with each other from having survived the war and been in a prison camp together—but I doubt that the wife would have displayed such a furious jealousy," he told me. "That's such a modern reaction. She killed them because she thought they were intruders."

This started our own little quarrel. Scott, an intensely focused businessman concerned mostly about *net worth* and *the bottom line,* thought my jealousy theory was inappropriate. In his estimation the concept of homosexuality was a modern-day psychological invention, perhaps because he had only recently discovered his own inclinations toward the same sex. Married for sixteen years, Scott had only been out as a gay man for four months when we began dating one another, so everything about gay life—and gay history—was new and a surprise to him. He was amazed to learn that Hadrian, Alexander, da Vinci, and

Lincoln all had gay pasts (not to mention quite a few of the ancient popes). "During the Civil War men used to dress up for the prison balls," I told him, when our argument about Peter Altemus and Will Ogden began. "They strung blankets around their waists for dresses."

"Then why aren't the ghosts seen in drag?" he asked. Scott was a no-nonsense sort of man. There was a logical explanation for everything. He saw nothing spooky about a squeaky door, for instance; it only needed to be oiled. (And he had all the husbandry skills our hosts lacked, a talent that resulted in our frequent weekend invitations to the country and Scott being peppered for handyman advice.)

"Technically, it would have only been one in drag, not both of them," I answered him. "And it would have only been occasionally, not a daily thing, especially since I doubt that there were a lot of prison dances or that Emma Altemus would not have noted that one of the men was dressed as a woman. So they appear the way they lived and died—soldiers embracing as lovers."

"They were probably embracing because it was cold," Scott said. "You've been reading too many gay books," he said. "Not everyone in the world is gay."

Though Scott was often amused by my anecdotes of gay history, he believed that I saw life from a narrow gay perspective. I worked as an editor for a gay news service that syndicated stories to gay newspapers, gay bar rags, gay blogs, and gay websites, and I enjoyed looking for historical precedents of current news items that I was reporting on. Scott never took my job seriously because in his estimation I didn't make a serious income from my gay work, certainly nowhere near his non-gay six figures. I believed that Scott diminished his homosexuality, hiding its existence as if he were ashamed of it. Scott was only out to a small circle of gay friends. Neither his ex-wife, his two children, nor his coworkers at the bank knew about our relationship, nor did Scott expect to change this arrangement anytime soon with new disclosures—a continual source of irritation between the two of us, because I always felt that he undervalued our relationship in comparison to those he had had with his girlfriends and his wife.

"Peter could have written Emma a letter about what it was like at the balls," I said, not ready to drop our little discussion or let Scott think he was off the hook. "*Dear Emma, the privates of our brigade had a ball last night,*" I began, reciting an imaginary letter. "*Some of the boys got themselves up in ladies clothes and were right pretty. A few of them even looked good enough to know better and I guess some of them did get things on with each other. I know I slept with my favorite pretty one. He kept me warm all through the night.*"

Scott arched an eyebrow at me as if I were the queerest man he had ever met. "Maybe you should direct your imagination toward solving global warming," he said. "The planet really needs someone like you to step up to the plate and make things better for *everyone.*"

Scott and I were close to breaking up the weekend of Arnie and Mitch's Independence Day party. The arguing had started the day before our drive to the country when Scott had introduced me as "a friend" to one of his coworkers we had run into at a restaurant near Times Square. We had spent the night together in the city at my apartment discussing the pros and cons of coming out. (Scott felt that he would be discriminated against at work; I felt that I was being discriminated against at home.) On the drive to the country the next morning, we had reached an icy stalemate and had managed to avoid each other during the

barbecue alongside Arnie and Mitch's new pool, talking with
the other weekend guests—mostly a couple who had driven up
from Washington, a closeted lobbyist and his very out and flam-
boyant boyfriend.

That evening Scott and I spent the night upstairs in "Emma's
bedroom," avoiding any intimacy. (Sex was the primary thing
that kept us together—usually we couldn't keep our hands off
each other, but that night we slept at opposite ends of the large
king-sized bed, deliberately shunning each other.)

The next morning the chill remained between us; the sky grew
gray with thick, dark rain clouds; and fearing that we would all
be trapped with one another in the country house because of
the miserable weather, Arnie proposed an outing to the nearby
movie theater, purposely to prevent his guests from escaping to
the city early and leaving him alone with Mitch.

Scott wasn't interested in seeing the movie—a romantic comedy—and decided to stay behind, saying that he needed the time
to prepare for an office meeting on Monday morning. In his own
way, Scott was as high maintenance as our hosts. He always
traveled with a cell phone, a Blackberry, a laptop, an iPod, and a
thin briefcase full of thick files. I didn't protest or plead for him
to join us on the outing to the movie, thinking he was hitting
the last nail in the coffin of our relationship. Before we left the
house, Scott had spread out his papers on the small café table
that was beside the giant hearth, flipped open his laptop, and
was contentedly at work, oblivious to the rest of us scrambling
for parkas, caps, and umbrellas.

It was raining when we left the house and, during the course
of our movie, the sky blackened and the rain came down harder.
Back at the house, Scott abandoned his work at the table for
short intervals to stand in front of the windows and look out
at the sloping countryside and the water puddling on the stone

path that led to the kitchen door. Alone, he was attuned now to all of the old house's quirky noises and motions—the tapping of the rain, the wind blowing sheets of water against the window, the creaking floorboards in the kitchen as he shifted his weight, the muffled, wet swinging chimes by the door. Scott was not a superstitious man and his practical mind was as far from wondering about the ghosts as it could be. He was thinking of the power of the rain, the solidity of the structure of the old house, how much it would cost him to put a down payment on a similar place, how he would redecorate it if he were its owner—how he would reorganize the kitchen counters and change the configurations of the guest rooms. Somewhere in there he imagined himself the resident owner and in that imagination he saw me as his partner in the kitchen cooking, reaching for a mixing bowl to make pancakes (his morning favorite) or experimenting with the color of margaritas (my favorite).

He returned to the table and his reading material and became absorbed in his work. Outside the sky darkened more, the rain continued, and Scott worked away. Upstairs a door in the house closed with a violent shudder, obviously pulled shut by the wind of the storm coming inside the house, and Scott was forced to look away from his laptop for a few seconds. Next, the overhead light in the kitchen sputtered and went black, and the laptop on the table slipped into the auxiliary power of its battery. Outside flashes of lightning flickered and a burst of thunder was so sudden and fierce Scott felt the table vibrate. He waited in the darkness for the power to be restored, for the lights to flicker and resume burning brightly, but when there was a dark quiet for several seconds, he sighed, then began to take note of where he was in his work, saving the documents open on his laptop. The kitchen was as black as night, the rain hammering the shingles of the roof and sliding down the gutters and windows and stones. For a moment he wondered where the circuit breaker was located in the house and realizing he didn't know, he folded his arms and sat back in his chair and waited a few minutes till the rain suddenly stopped and the black clouds blew away and the sun began to break through the darkness.

Light broke across a page of his notes first—bright and yellowish as if the morning had just arrived. The light widened over the table, then moved up his arms and chest and across his shoulders. For a moment he was conscious of the warmth of the sun and he squinted to adjust his eyesight to the fast rising light in the kitchen. The sunlight was accompanied by a strange burning smell—like that of wet wood and scorched hair—and Scott lifted his eyes away from the table to make sure that nothing was cooking on the stove top. Immediately, he felt a change in the kitchen and within himself and he knew he would see the ghosts before they had even appeared.

The trail of blood appeared first—initially as a crimson light against the wooden floor, then thickening and darkening into a river of red. His eyes searched out the edges of the red liquid, then followed it back across the room to where he sat by the hearth, and the deep red covered his legs and shoes. His heart was beating faster but he was not frightened or panicking. He was awestruck, in fact, as if he were watching a common phenomenon of nature such as the aurora borealis or comets streaking across the nighttime sky.

He thought about closing his eyes and avoiding what was next, but he refused to give in to fear. Beside the hearth, just beyond his shoes, a blood-soaked pile of straw covered with a tarplike cloth appeared, and then the shape of the bodies.

One man was lying on his back, his eyes and mouth opened wide with astonishment, the center of his shirt and chest blown apart with a bloody hole. The other man was on his side, his eyes closed in a wince, a blackened wound at his neck where the bullet must have hit.

As the sunlight moved further into the room, the pool of blood began to recede, as if time were reversing itself. The red edges shrank toward the hearth and the bodies and the smell changed, or, rather, disappeared. This was what worried Scott—he had not heard of this aspect of the legend.

But he didn't run away. Instead, he sat and watched the blood draw back, disappear toward the hearth and the men. When he looked again at the bodies, he saw that their positions had changed. They were lying on the tarp face-to-face, embracing each other as if to draw their bodies closer together for warmth. The wounds and the blood were gone and there was an unmistakable intimacy between the two men—one man's lips were nuzzled against the other's neck, reminding Scott of how he had liked to sleep with me, before our testy dispute. As he watched the two men sleeping, he realized that they were alive and breathing and there was nothing to be afraid of.

And then they were gone—vanishing as quickly as sunlight could fill the kitchen.

Scott was napping in the upstairs bedroom when we returned from the movies. The violent rainstorm had tumbled branches and leaves off the maple trees closest to the house, but had left the air cool and sharp and fresh. The power had been restored and I cleaned up the papers Scott had left on the small table beside the hearth, replacing them in the manila folders, and brought them upstairs to the bedroom, along with the laptop he had left behind. He stirred lightly when I entered the room, then rolled over and shook off his sleepiness when I was beside the dresser and placing the folders and the laptop near his briefcase.

"I'll do it slowly," he said. "The kids first."

"What do you mean?" I asked him.

"I'll introduce you to Wesley and Jennifer." Wesley and Jennifer were Scott's children, aged thirteen and fifteen, who lived with his ex-wife. "There's no sense in meeting Melissa. I'm sure she knows, but there's bad blood there already." Melissa, Scott's ex-wife, had pressed him hard for extra money and child support during their divorce settlement.

"Why the change?" I asked him, sitting on the edge of the bed.

He looked up at me, met my eyes, and said, "Don't be afraid. I saw the two men."

"What men?"

"The soldiers. The ghosts of the two soldiers."

The blood drained from my face and my mouth opened as I looked for some kind of response or appropriate form of sympathy.

"When the rain stopped," he said. "They were there, lying together by the fireplace. There's nothing to be scared about. I don't believe they'll cause us any harm. You were right. They were in love. I saw what they felt for each other. It's how I feel about you. They were simply two guys who felt like us."

Scott was right, no harm or misfortune or calamity came to him. Or us. The two soldiers were never seen again, nor have their remains ever been searched for in the barn or relocated to a more acceptable final resting place. But Scott and I often credit the ghosts of Peter Altemus and Will Ogden with turning around our relationship and creating a solid union between us, or so we like to tell our guests when we entertain them at our own country house. In the six years we've been together, Scott has come out to his coworkers at the bank, I've stopped pressuring him for proof of his feelings for me, and we bought a house down the road from where Arnie and Mitch continue to spend their weekends. Our country house is not haunted, except on those occasions when we invite Arnie and Mitch to join us for dinner. They arrive bearing quarrels and wounded feelings, though they always seem to be in better spirits when they leave.

THE RUSH OF LOVE

(THE TITANIC '70s BEFORE THE ICEBERG OF IRONY)

Jack Fritscher

t's Sunday night, August 19, 1978. I'm on Pacific Southwest Airlines, window seat 12B, returning to San Francisco from Hollywood-Burbank. With some urgency and some hysteria, I'm writing with a BIC ballpoint in blue ink on some scrap paper the stewardess found for me because of something that happened for forty-eight hours beginning Friday evening, August 17, 1978—something that happened like a movie I can remember in detail but am afraid I might forget.

What if memory is as fragile as my hot breath on the cold plastic window of this plane? What if memory is as liquid as that orange sun ball melting down into the far horizon of the Pacific? What if memory ends pretending it's metafiction in a gay magazine?

"Speak low when you speak love."

Imagine a night in late summer.

Kick Sorenson's maroon Corvette pulled into the drive of Dan Dufort's duplex on Willoughby Avenue south of Santa Monica Boulevard. We teetered on the southern edge of WeHo. For six months Dan had tried to get Kick and me together. "You're perfect for each other."

That sounded like the kiss of death, but it didn't stop any one of the three of us. It was Hollywood. Kick's car door slammed. Showtime. Dan met him at the door. Kick entered. He was better than any man I had ever seen. And I've seen stunners. His face alone, his body yet unwrapped, was perfect. Desire filled me. Everything I ever wanted to do with a man, to a man, or have a man do with or to me, flushed through my body. My eyes, and I'm not lying to exaggerate, came, looking at him. Never have I ever seen anyone who looked so noble, handsome, classic. The light in his blue eyes showed something more sensitive than I could ever have hoped for in a man of such physical beauty. He had no vanity. No attitude. He was what he was. He simply walked into the room and controlled the furniture, the radio, the breeze from the windows, everything, with his command presence.

I shook his hand and sat down, knocked out by his beauty, afraid I might turn him off by being taller. He and Dan stood in the center of the room and talked. I sat silent. Speechless. He turned and smiled at me. He said nothing, communicating everything. His eyes looked deep into me. Reassuring me. As if I already heard his heart say: "Here I am. Look at me. Look at what I was born with. Look at what I have worked at improving. I like it. You like it. It's all here. A gift to us. Let's share it. Let's enjoy it. Let's let go with no reserve. Let's get off on it together."

Humping his leg was out of the question.

He had dressed himself in fantasy gear he thought would

please me. He had tucked his blond body into an impeccably tailored California Highway Patrol motorcycle uniform: high-polished, calf-hugging black boots; the tan wool serge breeches bulging tight around his muscular thighs; the black leather police jacket, accessory belt with handcuffs, nightstick, and gun in the holster. His gold-framed cop glasses accented his tanned blond face. His hair was cut, groomed, and the kind of translucent blond that runs from black-blond to platinum. His bristle of moustache was authoritatively clipped, military style. He was a bulk of a man. No fag in cop drag. He understood perfect police dressage. He presented himself to me uniformed like a sculpture for an unveiling. I could tell he had an immense capacity for man-to-man fantasy play. He was, in fact, teasing me, and I was loving the foreplay. Dan had promised me a bodybuilder. Kick himself intensified the promise one step higher. He offered me my first reading of his physique as an ideal man in authority. He was perfect. He walked, flesh and blood and muscle, right into my platonic ideal of what a man should look like. He filled in all the blanks. He was my every fantasy. He was the kind of man I looked up at when I was a boy and thought, "That man. That man. That's the kind of man I want to look like when I grow up."

Kick terrified me. Never in this life did I expect the fulfillment of ultimate fantasy. But, I figured, if this sexual wish to dive straight to the heart of pure masculinity could be filled, what other wishes in life could come true? Most bodybuilders give no indication that their muscle can be used for anything but flexing. Kick, in his CHP uniform, went beyond decorative muscle-for-muscle's sake. He was an enforcer. He was a more real cop than most credentialed cops ever dream of being. He was a CHP recruiting poster.

Kick was the way a man should be.

He finally sat down opposite me. Dan fired up a joint. We talked about the heat and the smog and the fires along the freeway. He said he had never been to San Francisco. He asked me what the city was like. Dan sat back and grinned, listening to us making our way through the small talk with steady gains toward discoveries of everything we had in common.

Kick and I were not strangers.

We recognized we were old souls.

I masked what I was sensing, afraid he might not recognize what I already knew. I asked him how he came into muscle. I could tell he was natural, not a steroid freak.

"The summer I was twelve," Kick's voice was an easy lick of Alabama drawl, "I spent the summer with my uncle and aunt. They ran a filling station and café outside of Muscle Shoals." He grinned. "I didn't quite know then how much I'd learn to love that name. About the second week, I started noticing this trucker, a young one, came in everyday. He talked to me the way a grown man, who's not much more than a big kid himself, jokes around with a kid. I remember he had cut the sleeves off his flannel shirt. He asked me if I wanted to feel his arm. I reached up. Way up, I remember."

Kick raised his arm, smoothing his moves through the gestures of his story.

"I was such a little guy then, and he was so big. I wrapped both my hands around his bicep. For the first time, I felt how strong and hard and big a man's body could be. I hung on to his arm and he lifted me up. Swung me right up off my bare feet, up out of the dust. Face-to-face. I guess I pestered the shit out of him. Every day for the rest of the summer, without my asking, he let me swing from his arms, betting me he was strong enough to hold his flexed double-arm pose while I hung, my face to his chest, with both my hands on both his biceps. I could hear his heartbeat and I wanted arms strong as his. He bet me I could chin myself from that position." Kick grinned. "So I pulled myself up, the first time half-climbing his tall body. By the time summer was over, I was hanging from his arms and chinning myself up to his face. All that next winter, back in Mobile in my own bedroom, I stood in my white cotton underwear and started flexing my arms. Sort of posing the way boys do when they're home alone with a mirror. I studied my arms. I imagined them growing big and hard. Like his. You should have seen me. Squinting my eyes. Concentrating on them to make them grow. Moving to an angle in the old mirror that, when I caught the distortion just right, made my arms look bigger than they were. It gave me an image to grow into. I really worked at it."

He lowered his voice in a kind of manly modesty.

"I guess I have lucky genes. My mom and dad have good bodies. They said I was eating them out of house and home. The next summer I went back to Muscle Shoals about four inches taller and a few pounds heavier. But the trucker wasn't stopping by anymore." He leaned forward, rested his forearms on his thighs, raised his face, and looked me straight in the eye. "So that's how muscle turned me around. Especially on arms. They're big guns. That's where a man shines. Ask any guy to show you some muscle and ten-to-one he'll flash you a biceps shot. It's natural. If I ever compete, I don't care if I win or not, as long as I can take home the trophy for the best arms. So," he said, "that's it. That's how I got hooked on muscle."

Kick relaxed back into Dan's chair. He was smooth, slow, easy. Natural. The L.A. night was hot. In the duplex next door someone was playing the Eagles' *Hotel California*. I could smell his body heating up the leather of his police jacket. Sweet sweat was building up in him. His blond face glistened. He was in no rush to wham-bam. His discipline of slow Southern savoring kept him in cool control of his courting foreplay. He was intent on pleasing me. I put the brakes on my usual aggression and thought, *Let him play it as it lays.* He smiled at me, the way a man smiles when he's giving a new friend a gift. "I think I better take this jacket off," he said. He stood up. He reached for the zipper. Everything slipped into slow motion. His blue eyes squinted, sizing me up. Slowly, deliberately, he grazed the back of his hairy blond hand across his strong All-American jaw. His holster and gun and nightstick shifted. His shoulders and chest bulked huge under the creaking leather jacket.

One part of me thought, *Omigod, this is Hollywood!* Another part of me thought, *O God, this is Heaven!* The best gay sex scenes are half of both.

I was hooked to the tits. I couldn't, didn't want to resist him. I picked up his scene. I jumped on in. Words came tumbling from my mouth. Sex talk. Muscle talk. Man talk. Whatever. The scene had begun. I wasn't acting; nor was he. We were doing a number on each other. A real number. His hand slowly pulled the zipper down every tooth of the leather jacket.

"When you take it off," I said, "this will be my first look at you. At your body."

He smiled and pulled off the CHP jacket. Slowly. So slowly. That was his style, to move Southern-slow in the L.A. fast lane. First one muscled arm. Then the other. All his moves like the slow-motion Technicolor muscle movies of individual bodybuilders I watch every night clacking around on the Super-8 projector in my bedroom. He wore a tan CHP short-sleeve wool shirt. It bulged like armor over his chest. His gold seven-point star stood out on his left pec. His eighteen-inch upper arms filled the precisely tailored sleeves to bursting.

He was arms. Heroic arms. His thick forearms were downed with soft golden hair. His wrists were squared off in the classic way wrists are presented in men's watchband ads. His hands were perfect, defined, and powerful from gripping iron weights. His fingers and the backs of his hands were downed with sun-blond hair. His nails were clipped short. His arms, hands to shoulders, were arms to worship. This was no false god I had before me. In sex, I have few inhibitions. With him, I had none.

I was innocent beyond irony.

"You are," I said, "perfect."

He smiled, and something in the way he smiled assured me there was no vanity in him. Only an honest pride. He was a man who realized the body perfect for himself. He was a body artist, a muscle artist. Bodybuilding is a subjective sport, but he was as objective as any sculptor unveiling his work.

He kept his look straight on me. His fingers reached for the buttons on his police shirt. Again, slowly, deliberately, he opened the shirt: at his neck, down across his hairy blond chest, down the length of his washboard belly. He pulled the shirttails from under his belt. He dropped his arms down to his sides. He rotated his shoulders. The tan wool shirt pulled open over his chest and tight gut. He smiled at me, and slowly raised his left hand to palm inside the open shirt. I watched his hand run up the ripple of his belly and then smooth and cup his pectoral muscles. Already he had shown me more than I ever expected. He might have stopped and I could have flown back home happy. I've always loved seduction.

He peeled his uniform shirt deliberately off first one shoulder and then the other, revealing how wide side-to-side were his shoulders, how thick front-to-back was his chest, how wide were his lats under his shoulders and alongside his chest until they narrowed down to the tight V of his waist. He handed Dan the shirt, and stood before me, stripped to the waist, with his high-booted legs apart. The tailored lines of his motor-cop breeches clung to his thighs, swelled over his butt, and bulged at his zippered fly.

He was the incarnation of every mighty sexual hero I had ever conjured up in my erotic fiction. He was a vision stroked out of my one-handed study of hundreds of movies of bodybuilders. He was theology, literature, myth. He was Adam before the fall, Billy Budd in full bloom, a male god rising tanned from a blue sea with the vine leaves of a satyr wet in his hair. He was what I had always wanted. "You are," I repeated, showing ritual respect owed to an artist generous in sharing his creation, "perfect."

"You told me," he said to Dan, "that your friend liked muscles." Then he shined right on me. "Your friend," he grinned, "loves muscles."

"Your muscles. I love your muscles," I said. I had been lost and now I was found. "I love your proportion, your bulk, your definition. I love your symmetry. I love your *look*." I could not bring myself to say to these men that suddenly in my always terrified heart, I was a little less afraid of dying, which bullies had made me fear. Looking at Kick, I knew that if a being were to meet me on the other side of the squeeze of death, that if there were some sweet god, then what must eternal heaven be like, if god only looks this good, and this good feeling infusing my body lasts forever?

Dan sat silent as a sentinel off to the side, watching, stroking himself like a man watching a vision he knew would come true. The night heated up. Kick stripped in the spotlight set in the ceiling. His chest and abs glowed with thick blond hair. Long golden fur fleeced his thighs and calves and feet. His dick was more than most nylon posing trunks could pouch. "You can tell I ain't," he joked under his breath, "a hundred and eighty pounds of hamburger in a two-ounce posing brief." We played muscle sex until the hour before dawn. Kick posed and flexed under my oiled hands. Something more than sex, something like an understanding, was bonded between us. Dan knelt off in the corner stroke-watching the match he had made. He said later that Kick and I both were like beggars at an ecstatic feast, that we were perfect yin-yang, that gods need worshipers as much as worshipers need gods. I only know that I knelt before Kick for hours, rising up, stroking and sniffing and licking his body, eyeing his face close up, breathing his sweet breath, and for hours he posed, tireless, flexing arms and chest and belly and legs. He encouraged my sexual muscle-talk, following my words with his moves, as if I was scripting a scenario he had waited all his life to hear. We were smiles of a summer night, rising together up to that moment before climax, falling back, savoring the pleasure, rising up again, until our final mutual salute to triumphant masculinity.

Honest manliness is never half-revealed. When it's there, it's all there, total, present. Roman emperors could have tortured me to death, and with my eyes upon him, and his gladiatorial smile upon me, I could have been, even at his hands, the most joyous of martyrs. I could have died for love.

I knelt in front of him, between him and the mirror, sizing up the perspective of his muscle in the posing light. I had never before been ambidextrous, but I found my right hand reserved for myself. My left, as if for all my life I had been saving a virgin hand for stroking his hard-pumped muscle, palmed the contours of his body. I ran my left hand up his magnificent calves and thighs, not daring to touch his long hard rod for fear the muscle-worship would revert to purely genital sex. His dick was veined thick and heavy as his arms. I ran my hand up his washboard abs and stopped, flat-palmed, where his belly met his hard rounded pecs. We both dripped sweat. He looked down upon me, and for the first time our eyes locked into an affirmative understanding.

He raised his magnificent arms wide, never taking his eyes from mine, and rolled his broad shoulders. My hand on his upper belly felt his pecs harden and his abs tighten. He took a deep breath, and with all his might, flushing red, muscles pumped and veins roped around them, he intensified his look deep into my eyes, and pumped down tight and hard into the Most Muscular pose. His body quivered. Veins corded his massive neck. His jawline set hard. Heavy streams of sweat poured from his blond hair, down his forehead, around his eyes, along his lantern jaw-line, and dripped, I want to say like sanctifying grace, down on me. I looked deep into his resolute face. We hung in perfect balance: the adoring worshiping the adored. I knelt in high fealty to his presentation of ideal manhood.

Our eyes locked tighter in an unspoken energy of understanding. Hours before, we had left Dan behind, watching in amazement from the corner. Then we rose from the room, the mirror, the light, the clock. We moved to another dimension. We rose in that frozen moment to where the only clock was the one heart ticking between us. He held his body in the full locked-down power of his muscle armor. He was as graced with spiritual energy as he was with physical muscle. We were beyond words. My eyes looked hungrily into his, feeding back what he was giving out, circulating his energy back to increase his muscularity, to heighten our intensity, look to look, face to face, soul to soul. If there is a sweet god who meets me at death, and if his god-face is to reassure me, then let him look at least this good, and let that good feeling of that frozen moment be the beatific vision that lasts forever. Inside the moment of our intense look that held no secret from each other, I knew this was no false idol I had before me. At this moment, more than any spent kneeling before the Blessed Sacrament, I experienced true adoration.

"I worship you," my voice said, and it was my voice and not

my voice. Something that belonged to both of us was speaking. "I worship your muscles, your bodybuilder face, your muscleman soul, I worship all men in you. I honor all men in you." I fell into a litany of worship, stroking myself, rising slowly up toward his glorious face, shooting my seed over his veined thighs, and without pause continued on pleasing his insatiable satyr hunger. My pleasure in him pleasured him even more. My energy toward him caused him to pump out more male intensity. I hardened again. He displayed his double-biceps shot bringing his big arms to full flex. My hand ran up his body and held firmly onto his baseball biceps. I began to pull myself up to his chin. His eyes stared straight ahead into the mirror behind me, and, without touching himself, he shot hot rivers of seed and sweat down my face and chest.

Later, he said, "I felt I was taking all your energy. I usually pose alone. No one's ever followed along so well. I don't want to take anything from you."

I held my palms toward him. "Does a man holding his hand out to a fire ever feel he's giving rather than receiving heat and light?"

I wanted Kick. I wanted him soul and body. Through incarnated muscle, he opened his soul to me, for longer than an instant, and I, through my worshiping words, opened mine to him. We knew nothing about each other; we knew all there was to know. I wanted his spirit. My journey at long last ended. We had both shot in salute to what passed between us. It was not private parts, not crotches, not mere ejaculation, not sexual spasm. It was total whole-body orgasm. I wanted his Being. My homosexual searching had been no more than a physical trek across the geography of men's bodies to find this man's homomasculine essence through the medium of his muscle.

I push on my sweet-tooth of death. Sitting on this plane, flying home, I know I will never see Kick again. He will become one of those nights that on my deathbed I will remember. Sometimes perfect acts are better not repeated. We lay in each other's arms with the L.A. dawn already coming in the windows. "Sleep well, my fellow worshiper," he said. He kissed me. "I know," he whispered, "that you know what we know." I buried my face in his neck. He closed his eyes and drifted off. His breath, his slow even breath, in sleep was sweet. I can never thank Dan enough. Nor ever forgive him. Lying last night folded in Kick's huge arms, the thick hair of his chest warm under my left palm, I memorized the moment I know will never come again. I'll never forget lying in the tousled sheets with Kick, him sleeping, me knowing, with my head on his shoulder and my nose in his blond hair, the fact, the god-awful-fucking fact that in a finite changing world, no ticket is a round-trip fare. Life is a one-way ride through distraction to oblivion. This man, with these muscles, in whose arms I felt so shielded was a handsome, distracting way station on a journey I know we all must make alone. I slept and tried to dream that I might die before waking.

FUCKED ON KILIMANJARO

Jay Starre

Philippe couldn't recall what exactly had made him decide to undertake such a stupid challenge. His body ached all over, he was gasping for breath at least half his waking hours, and according to their guides there was worse to come.

Granted, the African landscape was absolutely gorgeous. Stark and increasingly barren, but with exotic plants scattered among the rocks and the unmistakable tracks of a lion around their camp that very morning, the slopes of the famous African volcano of Kilimanjaro were interesting to be sure.

But.

It was fucking exhausting, and Philippe was tempted to turn back nearly every morning. He was not a wimp, at least not most of the time. He loved hiking and had the thighs and butt to prove it, muscular and taut as a bowstring.

He would have given up except for one thing. Not his ego, not that at all. He had already gone higher on Kilimanjaro than most of the rest of the population of the world in just his first three days. One thing, and one thing alone got him up that morning and gave him reason to pack with a groan and push his aching muscles ahead, one step at a time.

Ralph was a lanky redhead, with serious blue eyes and a quirky smile, rarely offered. As the air grew thinner and the trail more difficult to negotiate, the man's perky buttcheeks hovered ahead of Philippe, beckoning him onward. He had taken to following just behind Ralph on the trail, and the redhead had seemed content with the situation.

Ralph often stopped while Philippe struggled to catch up; they would take a drink and gaze at the surreal landscape in companionable silence. Ralph had a thick Southern accent, which Philippe, born and bred in New York City, found adorable. But talking wasted precious breath, and neither had the energy to muster up conversation while hiking.

They shared a tent at night, which Philippe thought was a stroke of absolute luck. When he fell into his sleeping bag on the rocky, uncomfortable ground, the tall, athletically perfect redhead was snoring beside him.

It was Africa, but it was cold after dark on the slopes of Kilimanjaro. The flimsy tents kept out the wind, and fortunately the tour company provided small propane heaters, which Philippe and Ralph gladly lit once they crawled into their tent.

On the third night of their grueling ordeal, they lit their heater and nestled side by side in their thick sleeping bags. Philippe was content, Ralph already snoring beside him. The guy fell asleep almost instantly every night.

Philippe was supposed to turn off the heater after it had sufficiently warmed the tent. They had agreed on that, while Ralph woke first in the morning and lit it then so they could get up without shivering to death.

Philippe's mind wandered. He found himself half dreaming,

half fantasizing. Ralph's taut butt globes pumped steadily and provocatively before him, just out of reach. Encased in the flashy emerald shorts he liked to wear, each separate ass mound rolled and clenched and rose and fell, the deep divide between them promising hidden delights. Philippe contemplated that deep crack. Hairless, he was certain. A puckered hole. Pink. Tight. Willing.

Ralph's snoring diminished, then ceased. Next thing Philippe knew, he was sitting up and blinking sleep out of his eyes. It was the middle of the night and he heard Ralph's soft voice grumbling in the darkness.

"You forgot to turn off the fucking heater, Philippe! It's hot as Hades in here."

That sexy drawl stimulated his already bone-hard cock, which twitched nastily and bobbed up into the hot air of the tent. Philippe realized he had thrown open his sleeping bag in his sleep, with the heat he supposed. His exposed dick was stiff as hell.

It was too dark to see much of anything, but he could just distinguish Ralph's lean form as he crawled to the foot of the tent and turned off the heater. Without that small glow there was no light at all, and Philippe was thankful his rude erection wouldn't be visible to offend his new buddy.

Ralph crawled forward in the darkness. A hand groped Philippe's bare thigh. He jerked and gasped. The hand rose and fell again, this time landing right on top of his stiff cock. He yelped.

"What's this, Philippe? You got a woodie. Nice. Mind if I sit on it?"

Philippe's cock leaped in Ralph's fingers, not the least bit shy about broadcasting its emotions. Philippe, on the other hand, was unable to utter a single word. His mouth had gone dry in the heat and his body throbbed around the sensation of a hot hand now slowly pumping his cock. The image of Ralph's oh-so-awesome butt riding him was just too good to be true.

He was dreaming. He had to be. The thought released his tongue and voice. "Fuck yeah, Ralph. Sit on my hard cock. Fuck me with your hot ass."

Words Philippe had been dying to utter. If it was a dream, what was the harm? If he was rejected, he'd wake in the morning no worse for wear.

But the physical sensations bombarding him in the pitch darkness felt all too real. Ralph's thighs, lean and smooth, slid over his and settled down to straddle him. Satin-hot asscheeks, naked and firm, pressed into his lap.

It was no dream. Philippe gasped as he clutched for flesh. His hands found strong arms and pulled them forward. Ralph released Philippe's cock with a sexy Southern giggle, and then scooted up to sit right on it.

They both grunted at the connection of cock and crack. Philippe's stiffie throbbed between Ralph's parted buttcheeks, pulsing and twitching all along the deep valley where it lay mashed against his stomach and Ralph's grinding hips.

"Oh yeah, buddy. I'm gonna fuck you real good with my hot asshole. Real good."

The drawled nastiness was followed by more grinding, and Philippe had to feel that silky butt with his hands. He released Philippe's arms and searched farther, sitting up on his elbows until he discovered the objects of his desire.

Twin globes of heat. His palms cupped them as they writhed over his stomach. They felt larger in the darkness than he remembered them. Full and heavy and powerful. Sleek, clenching, relaxing, writhing over him as Ralph slowly humped Philippe's thick cock.

"You love that ass, I can tell. That's real good. Real fucking good."

Ralph's ass rose in the darkness, Philippe's groping hands following it, unable to relinquish the feel of those amazing mounds now that he had them in his grasp. He kneaded and stroked the big cheeks, probing into the spread crack and finding the sweaty crevice, even slicker and smoother. With Ralph's ass in the air, Philippe found the redhead's hole, and attacked it.

"Fuck, so sweet," Philippe grunted out as his fingers ran across the puckered slot and then settled on it.

"It's all yours. Hot and tight and ready for cock. You lick your finger and put it up there."

Philippe snorted, almost laughing at the nasty request uttered in that languid Southern drawl. But he instantly complied, moving one hand to his mouth and shoving a pair of fingers in it, working up a mouthful of saliva before removing the fingers with a slurp and returning his hand to that satin-hot buttcrack.

"How's this? Feel real good yet?" Philippe muttered.

His fingers, slick with gooey spit, collided with Ralph's wrinkled butt rim. The hole convulsed, twitched open and then swallowed those fingers whole. They sucked him right in as Ralph groaned, arched his back and sat down on the pair of invaders.

"Real good. Real fucking good," he gasped in the darkness.

The hole was alive with spasms and twitches. Philippe rammed deep and twisted, probing for prostate. Ralph wiggled his big smooth can over those fingers and began to fuck them, promising unbelievable delights for Philippe's cock once it replaced those fingers.

"Cock. You. Gimme some of that fat cock."

Ralph's face hovered close over Philippe, and the whispered words carried an urgency Philippe shared. His cock throbbed with need. The big bone jerked on his belly as it rubbed against an equally stiff cock his redhead friend was thrusting into him as Philippe's fingers twisted around deep inside him.

Now that Ralph's hole was spit-wet and fingered open, it was ready for cock. Ralph himself eased the way by spitting on his own palm and reaching down between their bellies to rub the gooey saliva up and down Philippe's stiff tool. Philippe yanked his fingers from Ralph's quivering hole and Ralph squirmed while propping up Philippe's cock so that the head was again rubbing into his smooth crack.

That hairless crevice was hot and slippery with spit. Philippe thrust up from the ground with his hips just as Ralph planted the head of Philippe's cock at the gooey entrance to his anal slot. They both wriggled together, moaning, then grunting as cock-head penetrated butthole.

Twitching anal lips parted, hot hole gulped. Philippe shoved and Ralph sat down.

The redhead was impaled. Philippe's mouth was wide open as he groaned loudly. His cock ached, entirely surrounded by pulsing anal flesh. Sphincter clamped over the root, while hot inner muscle quivered all around the fat shank and head. Ralph was breathing hard, his body rigid for the moment it took to accept all that girth inside his aching guts.

Then the redhead went nuts. Fingers reached down and clamped over Philippe's nipples, twisting and yanking as the Southern hottie began to ride the cock up his butt with slamming force.

Ralph rose and fell, fucking his ass and Philippe's cock with a slapping frenzy, his chunky buttcheeks smacking against Philippe's thighs and hips on every downstroke. The tight hole clamped around Philippe's cock like a heated vise, sucking him in then spitting him out with every rise and fall.

Philippe held on to those driving buttcheeks, squeezing and kneading them furiously. His back arched, lifting his chest into those pinching fingers as Ralph twisted his nipples like they were handles he was holding onto while he rode cock for all he was worth.

The redhead paused long enough to alter his rhythm, pulling almost all the way out so that only the aching head of Philippe's cock was trapped inside his snapping sphincter, then he began to grind his ass in circles as he fucked himself a little more slowly but just as deeply. He groaned and gasped, obviously feeling all the meat penetrating his guts and massaging his prostate. He fucked like a skank, riding and humping and squeezing and releasing. Philippe was helpless beneath him.

Philippe's nipples were on fire, a direct line of heated electricity arcing through his chest and down into his throbbing boner up Ralph's hot ass. Waves of fire emanated from both areas, cock and tits simultaneously. It was the hottest ass-fuck of his life.

Philippe had been fantasizing about this moment for days as he had groaned his way up the slopes of Kilimanjaro behind Ralph's sweet, pumping ass. Now that he was getting what he wanted, he sure as hell didn't want it to end. But orgasm couldn't be held at bay forever.

Ralph ripped it out of him. That squeezing, riding, twisting hole massaged and worked his cock so relentlessly, while those pinching fingers yanked his nipples so fiercely, he couldn't hold back. Holding in a scream with all his willpower, Philippe rose up off the ground and shoved deep into Ralph, then dropped down just in time to pull out and explode.

Cum shot out of him like a water pipe had burst, spurting over Ralph's heaving asscheeks. Fire in Philippe's nipples burned right down into his belly, balls, and erupting boner. He shook and gasped and thrashed all over.

Ralph released Philippe's nipples, which only made them throb all the more. As he was still squirting, Ralph scooted down on the sleeping bag and knelt between Philippe's thighs.

In the darkness, Philippe couldn't see what was going on, but he felt his thighs being lifted, Ralph's slim, smooth body moving again, and then the insistent throb of a very hard cock rubbing up between his raised legs.

"Now I get to fuck you. I've been thinkin' of your sweet butt for days and praying for a crack at it."

The words were whispered in the darkness, and Philippe's ears were ringing with the final, exhausted spurts of his orgasm. But he understood and, limp and willing, he spread his knees and offered up his own creamy brown butt for fucking.

And now he really got fucked. Ralph's cock was long and slim like he was, and stiff as an iron pipe. The head was like a gloved fist, though, as the redhead punched it right up Philippe's defenceless and quivering asshole.

Thankfully the cockhead was coated with a layer of spit Ralph had applied at the last minute before ramming it up Philippe's ass. That flared crown drove home, splitting Philippe in two and then searing him like a hot spear as it gored him to the balls.

Philippe's nipples burned, his asshole burned, and his chest burned. He gasped for air, partially because of the altitude, partially because he was so stuffed with cock. The ache inside him became another wave of intense pleasure that rose up to blast his hot nipples, still throbbing from Ralph's assault.

Philippe slammed back against the pile-driver dick up his butt, fucking himself as wildly and eagerly as Ralph had just done. Ralph's breathing was like a bellows in the darkness as he sucked in air with every pounding thrust up Philippe's tight ass. Hips slammed against asscheeks again. Hole massaged cock again.

Orgasm followed almost too quickly. The ache up Philippe's ass was a pulsing pleasure, and the fire in his nipples had become a soothing heat, and he could have gone on for much longer taking that lengthy fuck spear up his guts. But Ralph was fucking too fast and too deep, his cock drilling Philippe's tight hole in a frenzy that couldn't be resisted.

"I'm blowing. You got my load!" Ralph yelped.

The redhead pulled out and hovered over Philippe, his body tensed and then jerking as warm cum erupted from his cock to splatter Philippe's uplifted buttcheeks. Ralph sprayed Philippe's ass.

He collapsed on top of Philippe and both men gasped for breath. When he could speak, Ralph whispered in Philippe's ear. "I think I almost had a heart attack! Maybe it ain't safe to fuck at this altitude."

They began to laugh, their sweat-slick bodies thrashing together on Philippe's sleeping bag. But that effort had them gasping for air again and they finally settled down. They slept the rest of the night in one sleeping bag.

Philippe's determination to conquer Kilimanjaro was renewed, and three days later he stood beside Ralph for a photo at the peak. A sign beside them proclaiming Kilimanjaro Summit proved their conquest.

Naturally, the hike down was easier, but they still managed to work up a sweat. At night in their tent, mostly.

It could have ended there at the foot of Kilimanjaro in Africa, but Ralph went the extra mile. The redhead drawled out a sincere invitation to Philippe to visit him at his South Carolina beach house after they returned to the States.

Philippe took him up on it, and the New Yorker has been there ever since. They both get a kick out of telling people how they met—fucking, almost breathless, in a tent high on the slopes of Kilimanjaro.

GONE FISHING

Rob Rosen

S hit, shit, shit," I cursed, lunging, too late, for my cell phone
as it dropped, *kerplunk*, into the clear blue water of the toilet
bowl. I quickly retrieved the water-, urine-, and Clorox-soaked
device and flicked it on. To my utter dismay, a dead screen stared
back at me. Apparently, cell phones don't like to be dunked in
water, urine, Clorox, and whatever other chemicals were in the
bowl—which, of course, made two of us. I cleaned my arm and
the phone off, and tried to collect myself.

Only I was beyond collecting.

Normally, I don't talk on the phone while peeing. Normally,
I back up the information from my cell phone onto my laptop.
Normally, I don't have to plunge my arm into a toilet bowl at
two in the morning.

And, normally, I don't meet the man of my dreams at a gay
bar. Nightmarish men, yes, most definitely, and repeatedly, but
not dream men. No sir, no-how. Which is why I was standing
over my toilet bowl at two in the morning—I don't pee in bars,

being pee-shy and all—calling the man of my dreams, whom I'd met only three hours prior. In retrospect, the call probably could have waited until morning, but I figured he'd find it romantic that I called him so soon after we clicked. Okay, yes, he might have found it a tad desperate, as well, but I was looking at my glass, like my toilet, as being half full.

Anyway, I dropped the phone on the second ring, before anyone had picked up. *Kerplunk* it went, as did my heart, my stomach, and several other bodily organs. You see, his phone number, like all the other numbers, resided solely in my phone, unless it was backed up on my computer, which, of course, it wasn't—what with it being two in the morning and me just getting home.

I tried to remember his phone number, but to no avail. I dialed quite a few combinations of what I thought the number was, because, yes, besides being romantic, I was also, sadly, desperate; but all I got were a bunch of pissed off people who weren't thrilled at being woken up at two o'clock on a Sunday morning. And one guy who was seemingly as desperate as I was and promptly invited me over.

I declined politely. (Okay, I let him jack off on the other end first. I mean, I had woken him up, after all.) And then I sank to my knees, with head in hand, and cursed, once again, the evils of modern technology—in the olden days, a good three years ago, I simply would have gone out with a few Post-it notes and a pen.

"Okay, Chuck," I said, though, generally speaking, I didn't converse aloud with myself. "What are your options here?" I began ticking off a short list.

"Number one. Forget about him. There're other fish in the sea." Only my bait was quickly dwindling with each passing year, and the fish were getting smaller, stinkier, fatter. Besides, he was The One. I felt it down to my very bones.

I know that most guys have *a type* they go for: tall, short, hairy, muscular, young, old, white, black, a mix of all of the above. But my type has always been, up until now, elusive, for I sought the nearly extinct *normal* guy—not too tall, not too short, cute but not conceited, well educated, drug free, in decent shape without being too gymified, as I like to call it, with a good head on his shoulders, thoughtful, respectful, and, here's where it gets tricky, monogamous. Maybe I'd been fishing in the wrong pond all this time, because the desirable species of fish clearly wasn't biting.

Stuart, that's the guy's name, Mister Right instead of Mister Right Now, was all this and more. We met in a quiet corner of the bar. He was sitting alone, I was sitting alone, and we struck up a conversation. He'd never been there before, hating the scene even more than I did. Three hours later, with my heart going pitter-patter, I had his number and the most memorable, deepest, longest, lip-numbing kiss I'd ever had in my life. He was everything I'd been fishing for, plus a whole buried treasure to boot—the catch of a lifetime, in other words.

So, Number One was out. There was no forgetting about him. Even if I tried, I couldn't. Not those lips, not those sparkling blue eyes, not the soft hand that stroked my index finger as we sat there those several hours conversing.

"Two," I continued. "Keep dialing phone numbers until I reach him." I mean, I did have what I thought were most of the numbers firmly in my head. Eventually, I'd find him. Then again, I thought I had the phone firmly in my hand before it fell in the toilet, and look how that turned out. Besides, how many men could I bring to climax over the phone before that got old and boring? "Nix on Two."

I knew what Three was before I said it. But it was a long shot. I'd left the bar shortly before closing time. It was sure to be shut tight upon my return. And, even if it were still open, Stuart would certainly have left already. "Three," I groaned, putting my coat back on and trotting down the stairs and out to my car. "Back to the old fishing hole I go."

The bar was indeed closed, but several men who had lingered were headed to their cars as I drove into the parking lot and scanned it. And there he was, opening the door of a brand new, blue BMW—icing on an already delicious cake.

I hollered, I yelled, I screamed, "Stuart! Stuart, wait!" But I was too late or too far away. He screeched out of the other end of the lot, and out of my life. I tried to run after him, but running after a Beemer—you get the picture. He was gone in the blink of an eye.

"Fucking toilet," I said with a sigh, and headed back to my car, only to find I was no longer alone.

"Hey," a guy standing by my driver's side door said.

"Oh, um, hey," I replied, not in the mood to deal with anything or anybody.

"You looking for Stuart?"

My heart raced. Was I being offered a second chance? A lifeline? A blow job? At least my priorities were in the right order. "Yes, actually, I am," I replied, breathless.

"He's not worth it, you know."

Ugh. Again my stomach sank. Now what was going to go wrong? "Not worth what?" I asked, afraid of his answer but curious nonetheless.

"Dating. Chasing after. Fucking. Take your pick."

Um, sadly, those were my picks. I neglected to say this to him, though. "I just had to tell him something, that's all. But, if you don't mind me asking, why is he so low on your favorite person list?"

"We dated. Briefly. Guy's a dud. *Boring.* BORING. Doesn't go out to the clubs. Doesn't party. Would rather go to a museum than a mall. And worst, worst of all…" Oh god, what? What, in this guy's meager opinion, could be worse than someone who doesn't like to shop? "Worst of all, he's *monogamous*. Can you imagine?"

Bingo! *Bingo!*

"Ugh," I said, with fake disgust. "What a loser. So then, again, if you don't mind me asking, why did you date him, however briefly?"

"Guy's got a big dick."

Man, my karma must've been royally fucked. I must've killed kittens for a living in a previous lifetime to deserve this. "Yes, well, thanks." And then, with a last ditch effort, "Do you by any chance have his phone number, or address?"

"Sorry, bud, I never made it to his home, and I tossed his number a long time ago." He paused and leered at me. "But if it's a home address you're after, feel free to come over to mine."

Tempting as the offer was—*not!*—I declined. I was holding out for Stuart. Crazy at it sounded, when you know you've met Mister Right, you know you've met Mister Right. And if you can't reel in the big one, you might as well row the boat back to shore. Too bad for me the water was so rocky and my boat had sprung a leak.

I reached for the door handle, and then a thought popped into my already addled brain. A glimmer of hope. "Which museum?" I shouted at the guy, who was now at his own car.

"Huh?" he shouted back.

"Which museum does Stuart like to hang out at?"

"All of them. Goes to one every Sunday. Like I said, boring!"

I nodded my thanks and hightailed it out of there. "Every Sunday," I said, again talking to myself, which I hoped was only out of anxiety and not a new habit of mine. "Today is Sunday."

Now I only had one problem—well, one more on a growing list, besides having to buy a new cell phone. Did I mention I live in the city? New York City, to be exact. An awful place for fishing for normal guys—but not for museums. The city is awash in them. It could take endless Sundays for me to find him, if ever. What were the odds of going to the right one on the right Sunday at the right time?

Then again, I'd already beaten the odds once simply by meeting him in the first place. If lightning were going to strike twice, I would be standing out in the rainstorm with a big stick of metal held up in order to attract it. In other words, I wasn't giving up, not yet, not by a long shot.

Stuart was out there, somewhere, and I was going to find him.

I raced home, flicked on my computer, and Googled New York City museums. And there went that *kerplunking* stomach of mine again. There were dozens to choose from: the American Folk Art Museum, the Museum of Television and Radio, the Ukrainian Museum, the Queens County Farm Museum, the New York Transit Museum, the National Lighthouse Museum. You name it, there's a museum for it. And virtually all were open on Sundays. Thankfully, so was the Museum of Sex, which opened at eleven, and was third on the long list I compiled for the next twelve weekends of museum visits.

If I couldn't find Stuart, at least I'd brush up on my African, Tibetan, and Judaic art.

"No," I said, admonishing myself. "I will find Stuart. I will!" Great, not only was I talking to myself, but now I was shouting to myself. This must be how the other New York crazies got started.

So, with a new determination, I ate breakfast, showered, grabbed my list, and ran for my front door.

And there, on the other side, was Stuart.

"Stuart!" I practically shouted. Okay, I did shout it, which I think sort of scared the hell out of him. "What are you doing here?"

He backed up an inch, blinked, then said, "I was in the neighborhood and thought I'd drop by. The Children's Museum of Manhattan is just up the block. That's where I was headed."

I knew that. It was first on my list. My karma was back on track. "Um, yeah," I said, staring at him, wondering if I was dreaming. Then again, I still hadn't gone to bed yet, so that was unlikely. "But how did you find me? How did you know where I live?"

He smiled, a glorious, eye-crinkling smile. "Well, silly, you told me. Last night. Remember?"

I thought back...*Stuart, chitchat, blue eyes, hand-holding, address, kiss.* Fuck, I did tell him my address. With all the recent turmoil, I'd plumb forgotten.

"Of course I did. And here you are." I was almost at a loss for words, for there, truly, he was. In the glorious flesh, and just a scant few inches away from me.

"Oh, but you're on your way out. I'm sorry. I didn't have your number, or I would have called first. It's just, well, I wanted to, um, say hi, you know, again." He was nervous, and oh, so adorable. "Well, I won't keep you then. Maybe some other t—"

"No!" I shouted, scaring him back another inch or two. "I wasn't headed anywhere." He pointed to the coat in my one hand and the list in the other. I dropped both to the floor. "Oh, just to the store." I stared down at the long list. "To do some grocery shopping. For dinner."

The smile returned to his face, and a red flush rose up his neck and across his cheeks. "Yes, well, um, that's actually why I stopped by."

"To take me grocery shopping?" I was slaphappy from

exhaustion, or I wouldn't have asked such a stupid question.

"Um, no. Well, I could, if you wanted to. But no. I was going to ask if you wanted to do dinner. I know a great seafood restaurant nearby. If you like fish, I mean."

"Fish!" I'd have to stop doing that in the future, I knew, but at least I was no longer shouting at just myself. I stepped forward, and reached out my hand to his. "I mean, yes, I love fish. And, yes, I'd love to do dinner."

"Really?" he asked, taking my hand in his own and pulling me toward him.

"Really. And I love children's museums, too. All kinds of museums, for that matter. Tibetan, African, you name it."

And then the lips, those soft lips, were once again upon my own. And the perfect kiss from the night before was somehow miraculously bested.

"Well then," he said, when we'd come up for air. "Seeing as you don't need to go grocery shopping anymore, can I interest you in a trip to a museum?"

I squeezed his hand and shut the door behind me. "Lead the way."

Which he did.

And my fishing days were gladly and forever over.

VIVA LAS VEGAS

Max Pierce

I stood at the top of a grand staircase suitable for a classic MGM musical, but feeling less like Cyd Charisse and more like Debbie Reynolds: an eternal boy next door. Perennially cute, but seldom sexy. I forgot that sometimes cute wins over sexy.

It began as the *worst* date ever: a comic misadventure of epic proportions. If one was reading *TV Guide*, the log line would read something like this: Romantic Comedy; Boy travels to Sin City and finds nothing is as he expected yet discovers love in the process.

However, I hadn't the luck to read the log line. Three hours before I stood on that staircase, located in the swankiest hotel in town, I only knew I'd been invited on a potential romantic voyage and it was sinking faster than the Titanic, with no lifeboats in sight. Cue up Celine Dion.

Notice I wrote *potential*. I paid for my airfare but Tom insisted he'd pay for the hotel and we would be sharing a room. He was cute, I was cute, and it *was* Vegas, right? I'd read the literature.

This was my first visit to Las Vegas and I'd jumped at the chance to go. Showgirls! Roulette wheels! Ninety-nine-cent shrimp cocktails! If I were feeling particularly decadent, I might even smoke a cigar. So what if I didn't smoke? And the kicker: meeting Ann-Margret after her concert. Sexy, age-defying Ann, who'd rocked with Elvis, pined for Birdie, and was iconic enough to appear in animated form on "The Flintstones." Tom had a connection who had guaranteed we'd get backstage after the show. The time: early November, Halloween was out of the way but holiday thoughts hadn't taken over. The setting: Caesars Palace. And for the next eighteen hours, I rolled the dice and had the best date ever. And it wasn't with Tom.

Reality had kicked in shortly after I stepped off the United flight from Los Angeles, overnight bag in hand, and found I was being whisked *away* from the glittering Las Vegas Strip to the more moderately priced downtown area. Our hotel was no grand resort, more a glorified hostel with a room the size of a closet and the smell of an old humidor. It was perfect if you'd lost your pagoda at the Pai Gow table and needed a place to slash your wrists or swallow a handful of Seconal: precisely the reason why none of the windows opened. The presence of two twin beds in opposite corners, no less, squashed any idea of romance, as I'm not one for shoving beds together. Our $3.99 dinner in the hotel restaurant, a necessity due to our late arrival, made me eager to find a McDonald's—or a bathroom.

I had taken great care in dressing to meet Ann, perhaps a tad over the top, only to be informed by Tom that he had only secured *one* backstage pass. Setting a new record for the transformation from romantic possibility to platonic nobody during the cab ride between downtown and my dramatic Caesars entrance, I felt like the Christians being introduced to the lions. Suddenly trapped in a black-and-white RKO budget picture, I was a plucky hero pining for Technicolor, Cinemascope, and Stereophonic Sound. When a lonely boy knows he's different, but *doesn't* know there are at least ten percent more like him in the universe, and is raised on a steady diet of old movies, he can't help but aspire to glamor. I knew I didn't belong in downtown Las Vegas. I belonged in Caesars Palace, hobnobbing with the high rollers.

Ann, thank goodness, did not disappoint. Seated close enough to the stage that if she'd taken another tumble, as she did in Lake Tahoe in 1972, we could have caught her—and the eye of any press photographer in the pop of a flashbulb. After watching her sing and gyrate for two and a half hours, and guzzling one vodka-infused drink after another, my now-former date went around to the back with his original *Bye Bye Birdie, The Pleasure Seekers,* and *Bus Riley's Back in Town* posters, leaving me to my own devices. Exploring the casino, I plunked myself in front of a slot machine, accepted a complimentary cocktail from a woman dressed as an extra from *Troy,* and lost twenty bucks in ten seconds flat. Not sure how long Tom's assignation with Ann would take, and not having enough money to keep losing, I wandered out of the casino and into the hotel. In a rather obscure passageway linking Nero's all-night buffet, Cleopatra's disco Barge, and an exclusive restaurant named Bacchanal (which plugged toga'ed attendants massaging sacred oils into your neck while you ate), rose a marvelous staircase, all gilt rails and plush ruby carpet, stretching to where I wasn't sure; but my inner Nancy Drew had been activated and I was eager to find out. Never being one to pass on an opportunity to make life more like the movies, I climbed the stairs two at a time, paused at the top, whirled in a dramatic fashion, and began descending, arms outstretched, visions of Lana Turner in *Ziegfeld Girl* swirling in my head.

About two tap steps down, I remembered that Lana's character died in that film, so I wasn't drawing upon the most positive movie reference. Nor was Norma Desmond's close-up in *Sunset Boulevard* a good role model. *Hello Dolly!* and *Mame* were too obvious and far too queeny, even for a musical queen like me. I had no Rhett Butler to whisk me up, and there were too many steps to effectively re-create Bette Davis gunning down her lover in *The Letter*. I went back to Ziegfeld. Rewinding, I became Hedy Lamarr slinking downward to a chorus of "You Stepped Out of a Dream" that played in the soundtrack of my imagination. Halfway down, I eyeballed a cute guy in a black tuxedo at the foot of the staircase, looking like he stepped out of a dream. About this same time, a slot machine in the casino rewarded a Midwesterner with a jackpot.

Ka-ching!

"Yee-haw!"

The guy looked back up at me, and burst out laughing.

I mentioned earlier I had dressed a bit over the top: I was wearing a tux. And why not? I'd had one for years with no occasion to put it to use, until now. To me, Vegas means Sinatra, Steve and Eydie, and Bugsy Siegel, with well-heeled patrons tumbling from casino to showroom along the Strip soused on martinis and chewing cigars, garbed in fashions from Armani and Versace. Or in my case, Calvin Klein, whose tuxedo design I'd nabbed at a department store clearance sale. After partying into the wee hours, I'd expected Tom and me to stagger into our room and consummate the evening with a tumble onto the requisite circular bed while the mirrors on the ceiling reflected our every decadent act. Roll credits, end of story.

Of course, our hotel room was nothing like that, and even if there had been a second backstage pass, I don't think I'd have consummated anything. Right now, however, I was alone and in my element—glamor and just a hint of mystery with a stranger at the foot of the stairs. And whoever he was, he was about to join my movie, whether he liked it or not. Nicely draped in his own tuxedo.

Except he was still laughing at me. No longer Hedy Lamarr, I marched down the remaining steps, now in tough-guy Jimmy Cagney mode, hoping he wasn't a house detective about to bounce me from the joint.

"What's so funny?"

He said, "You look like you're having a good time."

"I am," I replied, as if I made a living walking up and down hotel staircases. At the last step, and to my amazement, I discovered I stood two inches taller than him. I didn't think there could be anyone shorter than me, yet he was, although what he lacked in height he made up in muscle, apparent from the thick forearm exposed as he extended his hand, and covered with a healthy amount of body hair of the Robin Williams variety. Behind us, another jackpot echoed in the casino.

Ding-ding-ding-ding-ding-ding-ding-ding!

"I'm Bill."

I shook his hand and lost myself in his eyes, which were hidden behind glasses. I'd popped my contacts in before I left the hotel, but left the all-essential drops in the room. The smoke in the air was making me squint, and I wondered if Caesars' amenities included an all-night drugstore.

"Did you see Ann-Margret's show?"

"Yes. I especially liked the number where she sang and danced with her old film clips." Oddly, I now pointed out, Ann had looked younger now than she had in her *Birdie* days. After saying that, I hoped Bill didn't think I was too bitchy.

"Have you seen the pool?" It was a charming non sequitur.

I shook my head and we, two penguins, walked outside. The

deserted pool was oversized, like everything at Caesars (except my new acquaintance), and decorated in a *Roman Holiday* motif. The fresh November air, dry as vermouth and windy and warm, had the same effect on me as a bushel of raw oysters. I eyed Bill much like a cat does a canary.

"Where are you from?" we both said at the same time.

"Los Angeles," we both answered.

This was an incredible run of luck. Had I not been so interested in continuing my conversation with Bill, I knew I could have run in, plopped a hundred on the roulette wheel, and doubled my bet.

"My friends are backstage getting her autograph." Bill said.

With that, I might as well have been Cinderella—wearing a watch with a dead battery—who hears the village clock strike midnight. Tom! My date-in-name-only. He had paid for the show tickets. Yikes.

I was glad the pool area was discreetly lit, as I knew my eyes had bugged out. "My…friend is probably looking for me."

"Boyfriend?" Bill asked.

I shook my head. He too had mentioned friends. I prayed that was plural.

"Boyfriend?" I queried, holding my breath.

"No. Let's go back in." And there, in the stillness, beside the shimmering pool reflecting faux-ancient columns and pseudo-classical statuary, with the lights of the Strip illuminating the sky above us in a Technicolor rainbow, Bill leaned over to kiss me, and there was nothing faux or pseudo about it. Bingo.

Okay, so he wasn't *that* much shorter than me.

During the walk back into the casino, my sense of honor attacked me. I had come to Las Vegas with Tom, and even if things hadn't worked out, manners dictated I should remain with him. I'd been on the receiving end of being dropped more often than

I cared to remember, and it wasn't a pretty feeling. The polite thing, the honorable thing, would be to get Bill's number and call him later.

Or I could tell Tom *See ya* and drag Bill to the nearest poker table. We'd fit easily under the green tablecloth.

For years I'd been the good boy with the straight A's. I was entitled to a little selfishness. And if Bill turned out to be a mass murderer, well, so be it. It wasn't the first time I'd gambled on romance and come up short—make that lost.

The casino was swarming with activity, except around Tom, who stood tapping his foot impatiently where we had parted earlier. What a difference twenty minutes can make!

"Where have you been?" he said, eyeing Bill as if his lamb had come back to the pen accompanied by a miniature wolf.

I can be pretty quick with my back against the wall. I did a double take. "Oh! Why, this is...Bill. He's from...Los Angeles. Small world, isn't it? Bill, don't you know...Tom?" I hoped this cocktail party chatter made it seem as if we were all old friends.

I needed to go no further with my charade. Bill's friends Ray and Greg, also tuxedo-clad, popped over clutching programs. Never before or since have I felt as if I'd fallen through a film screen and right into a classic screwball comedy. If Carole Lombard and William Powell strolled up, I would not have been surprised.

"I've been invited to go with some of Ann's friends—" Tom said, his voice fading out after *go*. Just where they were going escapes me now. Maybe Ann-Margret herself had seen Tom in the front row clutching his posters and was spiriting him away for a private screening. Whatever the destination, I knew providence was removing Tom. I needed to offer a novena, at my earliest convenience, to thank the patron saint in charge of romance.

"I have my key, so I'll see you back at the hotel," I answered, hoping *back at the hotel* meant tomorrow around the time we caught the cab to the airport. It probably was not the most tactful dump, but I didn't care. This was a magic moment, and I was going to hope for a royal flush. I could blame it on the staircase and the Stoli.

With Tom conveniently removed, I got acquainted with Bill and his friends. He was the chief financial officer for an upscale Century City firm. Ray was an entrepreneur who owned a variety of successful businesses. Greg was Ray's boyfriend of the moment, and didn't appear to have any job other than placating Ray, which appeared to be a full-time job. Ray wanted to play baccarat, so we went into the high roller area, the one cordoned off with velvet ropes. We were ushered through by burly yet impeccably groomed guards as if they had been waiting for us.

Ray lost five hundred dollars on his first bet. As I saw him toss another chip down, my mind reeled with the thought that his chip could pay my rent. To my relief, Bill was much more frugal with his money, and we watched Ray lose, and lose, and lose. In fact, Ray and Greg became so absorbed in their game that we were able to casually fade into the background.

Bill asked if I was hungry and I nodded, so we took the moving sidewalk out of Caesars to the street, then strolled over to the Flamingo. The wondrous thing about Vegas is that if you get tired of ancient Rome, just nearby are Paris, Venice, Egypt, Manhattan, and so on. The Flamingo was the brainchild of Bugsy Siegel, who, it is said, buried a few enemies in the hotel flower garden. We had a late supper at the Peking Market, a bustling restaurant replete with an enormous aquarium, lanterns, roasted ducks hanging in the window, and mandolin music echoing off the teak walls. In the excitement of the evening, the ill effects of my cheap dinner had worn off, and having been fueled only by vodka for the last three hours, I was starving. But a bowl of egg drop soup, followed by a platter of moo goo gai pan and combinations of beef, broccoli, and Szechwan shrimp restored me.

We left the Flamingo and went to the MGM Grand. This was my kind of hotel: I could spend hours looking at the photos of the stars. I kept an eye on my camp-o-meter; no sense scaring Bill off by reciting movie lines for the balance of our evening. After a stroll through, we skipped out and explored the Imperial Palace. The Palace was a little down market after the pizzazz of Caesars, the MGM Grand, and the Flamingo, but we did have some clever drinks served in little ceramic skulls. We talked the whole time, about our jobs, our families, and our dreams as if we'd known each other for years and not just an hour. I'd never met someone I connected with so quickly and so well.

By three A.M., after such a glorious evening, there was no way I was going back to my closet-sized cigar box with its twin bed. Bill was staying downtown too, but at the Golden Nugget, with its clean-smelling rooms and decidedly more upscale atmosphere. I walked him to his room and as he opened the door, he shyly looked at me. The room was large and well air-conditioned. There was no mirror on the ceiling, and the bed was square. But it was California king-sized. We tossed our tuxedos and snuggled under the covers, but not before making sure the heavy drapes blocked out the approaching sunrise. I was glad I'd taken a bet on love. *Roll credits.*

WHAT THE EYE REVEALS

Jason Shults

We'd booked the last available flight from LAX, wanting to milk the weekend for every last drop. But that was before the actual trip. Now it's three A.M., Monday morning, and both of us have school in less than six hours, myself as professor and Bob as student, though at different colleges. I teach math at the university, and Bob's studying anthropology at the community college. Or maybe it's agriculture. Something beginning with *A*, anyway.

We throw the bags on the bedroom floor, strip off our clothes, and climb into bed. As always, I'm aware of the differential in mattress shift, his long lean body barely making a dent in the foam and coils, while my somewhat rounder, denser (and yes, older and balding) form sinks like a doomed soul toward the center of the earth. Bob reaches away to turn off the nightstand lamp, and then rolls toward me, drawn there by gravitational forces. His arm flops across my chest, and his familiar scent—a scent vaguely reminiscent of hay and honey and freshly-baked bread, the homespun scent of a farmhouse, of a gentle child-hood—fills the air around me. For a moment, the underbelly of his arm scratches itself on the coarse black hair of my chest. I lean forward, trying to sniff Bob's arm, trying to gain more immediate access to his pheromones. I can smell my own body, too, sweat-caked with travel, but the stench fails to overtake the honey and hay. Even in darkness, Bob is golden, overpowering. I breathe deeply, but the chemical attractors can't completely quash the residual bitterness between us, a low-grade mutual enmity picked up during our trip to L.A.

"Julius Caesar, maybe," I say, lying back against the pillows.

"Mm?" says Bob.

"Me. In a previous lifetime. Probably Julius Caesar."

"And who was I?" Bob says.

Brutus, is the answer I want to give, but I don't. *Backstabber, usurper of power. Or Cleopatra, betrayer in love.* What I say instead is this: "My faithful slave girl, of course. Secret love of my life, the only person faithful to the very end." I sigh dramatically, trying to lighten the dark air. "But forgotten in the cruel crush of history."

"At least *you* remember me," Bob says. "That's all that counts, right?"

I sneer into the darkness, but of course Bob can't see it. I almost say it aloud, one or the other of the things I'm thinking. Brutus. Cleopatra. But before the words reach my throat, I hear Bob's soft snores, feel his arm relaxing against my chest, feel myself sinking even lower into the bed. My own breathing eases. Images come, unbidden. I'm lost in time, slipping into a world I've invented for someone else's sake, for the sake of a relation-ship that I feel hasn't quite lost its last momentum. A slave girl, blonde and slender, stands above my bed waving palm fronds. A cooling breeze comes from nowhere, and I lie there, pampered, the taste of grapes in my mouth, the taste of honey, the taste of freshly baked bread. Past and future, reality and imagination, melt, meld into one another, love and betrayal becoming just two ways of saying the same thing. Later on, I sleep.

The next morning, I'm not quite myself. For one thing, I've had dreams, unrecallable in entirety, grasped only as fleeting images, emotions. They linger throughout the morning and well into the afternoon, these internal tropes do—slaves and tricksters, feelings of lust and exposure—climbing like monkeys on the sleep-deprived circuits in my skull. I rote my way through a Calc One class, stumble through Introductory Topography. The students, all of them ridiculously young, seem not to notice my sudden ineptitude. Words come from my mouth, chalk-lines squeal from my fingertips, and none of my bleary communications are any less comprehensible than usual, apparently. By three o'clock, I begin to think I might just make it unscathed through this dreadful, waterlogged day.

When the bell rings, the last cattle call of the day, I amble into the classroom. It's a small room, a small class, just six students seated around a rectangular wooden table. Special Topics, the class is called, a theoretical title for a purely theoretical class. In here I'm not the teacher, but serve instead some more mundane function: class monitor, or maybe figurehead. Untrue, of course, but it often feels that way. Only the best and brightest ever make it this far through the program, and mostly they manage on their own. But in the fifty-minute sessions, three times weekly within this room, just hearing the students theorizing, brightens up the remainder of my otherwise backsliding and bleak career. I'm continually surprised by their imaginations, and this helps me survive, in some fundamental way. Questions pop up from nowhere, the students always looking for the

envelope's furthest edge. It's my job only to show them where
the edge lies, and why it lies there. Occasionally, I'm useful.

The special topics change from semester to semester (chosen
by secret ballot at our first meeting). For this class, the students
have chosen to prove the existence of zero, a not unsolvable
proof, but approaching impossibility, straining against the limits
of the human mind.

I call the class to order, but after that I drop my tired body
into a chair, sit back, watch as the nimble-minded youngsters
toss ideas like Nerf balls around the room, squeezing them, re-
shaping them, sometimes tearing them to bits. The discussion
becomes heated when one student, having worked quietly while
the others talked, throws his hands up, stands suddenly, and
nearly screams, "It *doesn't* exist! Of course! Of course! How
can a nullity exist at all? Don't you see? Don't you see? It *can't*
be proven!"

He's hastily attacked from all sides, indicted, ridiculed, and
rightly so; the problem strains the limits of reason but doesn't
break them. The answer exists, somewhere, waiting to be found
again. The young man, all of maybe nineteen, grows red in the
face. Instantly he becomes obsessed with his eyeglasses, pushing
them up his jutting nose, pushing them up again when they immediately slide down. He tweaks the earpieces at his temples.
Repeatedly, he pushes his longish brown hair behind his ears,
from where it promptly falls forward again, into his face. He
says nothing, only gawks spastically at those around him. He's
a fidgety mess. He seems struck dumb by the reactionary storm,
and I feel badly for him, but also I feel energized by the vigor of
the attack. Such fervor, such ire, and all of it caused, literally, by
nothing. I can't help but laugh.

Trey Rothman—the boy's name—runs from the room. I follow. He's gone, invisible, by the time I reach the hallway, but I

hear the echoing clunk of the men's room door shutting at the far end of the hall. Wearily, not really wanting to play the part of father or therapist, I trudge down the hallway, pull open the bathroom door, and go inside.

Trey is leaning over a sink. I can see the denim fabric of his baggy jeans shuddering at the knees, the slight motion fueled by anger, fear, embarrassment. I walk toward him, place a hand on his bony shoulder and feel that it, also, trembles.

"Nothing to get so upset about," I say, as gently as I can. I've never quite understood the rules of pathos, of empathy. I pat his shoulder twice before letting my hand settle onto it again.

"Even you," he says, shaking his head slowly back and forth. He looks up, into the mirror in front of him, turns his eyes so that they meet the reflection of mine. In a soft, low voice, he says, "You laughed at me."

I take my hand away from him, stick it into my pocket. I stand back, search for inspiration in the blank green tiles of the walls and floor. A student walks into the bathroom, sees us, and promptly turns to leave. I wait until the door clunks shut again before I speak. "I was laughing at the situation, Mr. Rothman. I wasn't laughing at you. Trey? A thousand other mathematicians have made the very same mistake you made, and every one of them has been attacked in precisely the same way. You should consider yourself in good company."

"So it *was* a mistake, what I said?"

"A good mistake. A mistake that's on the right path." I slump, trying to seem sympathetic. Maybe I really am being sympathetic, maybe this is what it feels like, I don't know. I lean against the wall of one of the toilet stalls and press my naked scalp against the cool steel divider. "When it's all said and done," I tell him, "I'm willing to bet that you'll be the one to solve the zero proof."

He turns then, and faces me, standing upright. Earlier he'd laid his glasses on the lip of the sink, and now he puts them on again, adjusts them, crosses his arms over his chest. "You really think so? You're not just shitting me to make me feel better?"

"I don't know how to make people feel better, Mr. Rothman. It's not in my repertoire."

We stand in silence a moment longer, until I begin to think the crisis has been finally and ultimately averted. But Trey speaks again, verbalizing the second half of a thought.

"—Because I don't get the whole symbol thing. I mean, how do we get from *things* to *symbols* of things. You've got one thing, and then you've got the symbol for it. Where does the *meaning* come from? The numeral zero and the nothingness. There's no bridge between them." He opens his arms and flutters them in the stale, damp air. "It sounds so stupid, but…"

"It's not stupid. You're just going too far. We're talking mathematics here, Mr. Rothman, not Wittgenstein. You have to think about the problem on a more practical level. You've jumped ahead. You just need to slow down. Back up. Start again."

He thinks about what I've said, and then nods definitively, but says nothing. A ghostly smile passes over his rosy, pimpled cheeks, his lips twitching almost imperceptibly, his eyes quickening with a sudden light. And then it's gone, and an infinite seriousness overtakes him. He moves forward, toward me, removing his glasses yet again, placing them deftly on the sink behind him. He reaches out, touches my upper thigh with one hand, grasps my elbow with the other hand. And still he comes closer, until my nostrils prickle with his sweet and rapid peppermint exhalations, closer, until I can feel the radiant warmth of his skin on my skin, until I can see the pupils of his eyes, dilating, and the fractal patterns of the green-and-gold irises, trapped like feathers beneath tiny domes of glass.

"We'd better get back to the others, Mr. Rothman," I say.
He kisses me quickly, and we leave.

After class, Bob and I go shopping for our supper. At Delicacies—an overpriced market in an upscale strip mall—we pick up a frozen mushroom-and-spinach lasagna, a pre-made salad, a bottle of cheap but decent wine. Outside, once we reach the car, I begin prattling about something or other, surface-level nonsense I'm mouthing to try to mask my underlying distress. I'm sure that Bob will notice the something wrong, that he'll see Trey Rothman's advances scratched indelibly into my very being, an acid etching, detectable by some new way in which I move or speak, some new gesture or facial tic. I pile two brown bags into the backseat of the car, and manage, for the first time that evening, to venture a look directly at Bob. He's noticed nothing, isn't even looking at me. His sight is aimed dreamily at the Pets-a-Lot, the mall's monstrous anchor store, a hundred yards away.

"You ever wanted a dog?" Bob says.

"Not particularly."

"Cat, canary, goldfish? Anything?"

I shake my head, and then, because Bob is still aimed Petsward, I say aloud, "I don't see the point."

"To have something to love you unconditionally? You've never wanted that?"

"I thought that's what you were for, what I'm for. Love and whatever."

"Unconditionally?" he repeats.

"Sure," I say.

Finally he turns to look at me. "Really?"

I lock the car, grab Bob's arm, and lead him toward the gaping maw, through the sliding doubled jaw, into the shrieking, cackling, gullet of the beast.

Puppies, kittens, fish. Gerbils, hamsters, guinea pigs. Bob examines each specimen as if his life depends on his choice of pet. He taps on the glass, squats, peers into the shadowy recesses of bedding and tiny toys, considering each animal's potential, like a dowser might make his way slowly across an open field, divining where the water hides. There in the store, dogs galumph against their owners' leashes, straining to chase other dogs, straining for no reason at all. Passing with their owners through the narrow aisles, hounds and purebreds press themselves against Bob's legs—Bob's legs but not mine. They slobber on his pant cuffs, sniff at his leather shoes, before being dragged away.

"Saint Francis," I say.

Bob's looking at an empty rabbit hutch, a giant specialty model made for people whose love of bunnies goes way beyond the norm. It stands maybe five feet tall, six feet long, four feet deep, perched high on curving, claw-footed legs. The frame is made of carved maple, the wire fencing coated with clear and hi-tech nontoxic polymer (or so the attached flyer says). There's a litter tray of galvanized aluminum beneath the wire flooring; a set of wooden shutters attached to the hutch's front can disguise the fact the thing is a cage at all.

"Jesus," Bob says with a whistle.

"Saint Francis," I say.

"What?"

"I'm thinking," I say, "that maybe you were Saint Francis in a previous lifetime." A loose bird flies through the ceiling rafters overhead, distracting me momentarily from my thoughts. When the bird perches, I return to what I was saying. "This animal thing you've suddenly hooked on to. Where'd it come from?"

"I grew up on a freakin' farm," Bob says. "Sometimes I miss the moos."

Bob shuffles a little way down the aisle, touching everything as he goes. Hamster wheels, gerbil treats, fluffy little bags of batting designed especially for rat beds.

"Or maybe you really were Jesus. It's possible, I guess."

"Forget about it already," he says. "It didn't mean anything. For god's sake, it was just some guy in a turban trying to make an extra buck."

"Twenty extra bucks," I say.

"Whatever."

"And it doesn't bother you at all, what he said? You don't even see the possibilities, the possible wrongness?"

"I believe in what I see in front of my face," Bob says. He holds up a miniature log cabin, a countrified mouse-house, and then sets it back on the shelf. "Not what some guy on Venice Beach tells me about who I was in a past life. Or who you were."

"I was nobody, apparently."

"You're here now."

"Our karma's not connected," I say, repeating what the turbaned psychic had said less than forty-eight hours ago. "I'm no good for you, Bob."

"You don't believe that."

"I believe that you believe it."

"I don't," Bob says.

"But you've been infected with the idea. That's the way those people work, planting little seeds of doubt. Why do you think I never read my horoscope? I want to live my life, not worry about *how* I should be living it."

"So here I am, living my life," Bob says. He spreads his arms wide, marches in place. "See?"

"But you're wondering if he might, just might, have been right. Aren't you? Aren't you?"

Bob closes his eyes, squinches his face into something close to anger.

A family—a blue-collar dad and stay-at-home mom and two girls of maybe four and five years—appears from nowhere. They gather around the rabbit hutch, ooing and ahing. The girls play with the latch until they manage to open the hutch's wide front gate. The mom and dad whisper to one another, pointing, stroking the smooth wood, plucking their fingers against the insulated wire mesh. I hear the words "layaway" and "Christmas," and then the family disappears again, all of them but the smallest girl.

Bob has vanished too. I choose not to follow him. He'll fume for a while before deciding to come back, before deciding that he has no choice but to indulge my silliness, to soothe away my self-doubt, provide for me a rational balm by torturing his argument into some logical, emotionless set of axioms I'll be able to understand. It's happened before. It's always happened before.

The little girl is cooing like a pigeon. She's got the hutch's door open, her head inside it, and is shaking her hair wildly like an epileptic. I'm not certain if I should be concerned or not. The parents are still nowhere to be seen. At the back side of the cage, I crouch, look in through the mesh. She seems to be okay; only playing. A playful mood hits me as well, I'm not sure why, and I decide to go along with it. I cluck at the girl, bring my fingers to the wires, thumb and forefinger pinched together as if I'm holding bread crumbs or tasty grubs. I'm beginning to feel ridiculous, superfluous, like an old lecher, when she finally takes a step forward, hand and knee. She smiles, catching the thread of the game. She rocks back and forth, teasing.

"Here pidgey, pidgey, pidgey," I say.

The little girl laughs, scooches herself forward until her entire body is held within the hutch. As her foot slips in, the laces of her sneakers catch the door, which closes behind her. I hear the latch drop firmly into place.

"You're sleeping with somebody," someone says. It's Bob. He's looking at me through the mesh, disgusted. For a moment I'm not sure what he means. I'm only thinking how bad it looks, me here with this little girl locked inside a cage. But Bob calmly opens the door. The girl climbs out and runs off, skipping into the bowels of the fluorescent monster.

"Jesus, Bob," I say. "I'm not sleeping with anyone."

"You want to, then. It's the only thing that makes sense. Why you're so hung up on this karma crap. You want me to leave you."

We both stand, looking at one another over the top of the hutch. I try to mimic his expression of disgust, but can't quite manage it.

"Let's go home," he says.

The previous weekend, we'd gone to Los Angeles for the Warhol Retrospective at the Museum of Contemporary Art. Bob had seen an advertisement somewhere and nearly begged me to tag along with him. I'd never been much of a Warhol fan, but I enjoyed Bob's company, especially when we were alone together in crowds. I don't know if I'd call it vanity, but I got a thrill out of watching people watch Bob walk by, looks (gapes) I'd never attained myself, no matter how primped and pomaded I was, even back when I'd had hair. And more than that, I liked Bob. I enjoyed being in his company, in crowds or otherwise. We'd been together for nearly four years, and I still found him as appealing as ever. He was simple, straightforward, honest, a counterbalance to my hidden dark side—a dark side which never really expressed itself, but which nevertheless lay in wait for the appropriate moment to lunge forward and ruin my life, as I was sure it someday would. And Bob was a tether to *goodness,* an anchor, a chain linked to the childhood virtues; Bob was faith, hope, and charity incarnate. Truly.

Saturday was Warhol, all day. Uneventful. Subdued. Muted whispers in a white space. That evening at dinner, Bob raved about the exhibit, but I couldn't see the point. Dead people in primary colors. Soup cans. Brillo boxes. But I enjoyed Bob's excitement. At the restaurant, I listened to his chatter, watched as linguini got slurped between his grinning lips.

Sunday we went to Venice Beach. The day was a pleasant one, midseventies in mid-March, a few cottontail clouds in an Easter-egg sky. Around us were the smells of a hippie carnival—patchouli, funnel cakes, pot smoke—carried in a sweet, salty air that made you want to drink deeply of all the smells. The motion of the people against the stationary backdrop of the beach, ocean and sky, was almost joyful. And the variety of the people themselves—their attitudes, performances, talents, and lack thereof, their states of undress—was dizzying.

Bob stopped at every other booth along the paved walk, eyes wide and jaw dangling. He giggled more than I'd ever heard him giggle. By noon he'd gotten two temporary henna tattoos (a Celtic cross on his right wrist and a jagged tribal armband around his left bicep). He'd stripped off his shirt to show them off. And he'd filled his belly with fifteen kinds of sugar.

"Your faces show your past, my children! The future is in your eyes!"

At a booth down the walk, a showman of some sort barked out a pitch.

"See the unseen, my children. Know the unknown! Twenty dollah! Only twenty dollah to know it all!"

Bob shouldered his way through the crowd, careful not to corrupt the intricate traceries of the henna armband. I followed in his wake.

"So you want to know your future, my child?" the barker said. "You want to know your past?" He was holding out his arms, waving us closer. He wore nothing but a turban, blue as the sky, wrapped around his head, and around his waist a cloth like a diaper. His tan looked fake, orangey, but he couldn't have faked the emaciation: twiggish arms and legs barely thick enough to stand on. His belly pooched out and caved inward at regular intervals.

Bob was holding out his hand to me, wanting money.

"What?" I said. "You're not really thinking about doing this."

"Sure. It's a holiday, for Christ's sake. Try to be fun for once."

I handed him the money but didn't stay around to watch.

I wanted water. Clear, clean, simple water. Not fruit smoothies, not colas, not lattes, espressos, or hyper-sweetened teas. I was beginning to feel coated, inside and out, by grime. I was sticky with the place and wanted cleansing.

When I got back from the water fountain, Bob was frowning. The psychic/guru/diaper-man was frowning. The two were seated cross-legged on a dark red rug on the sand, facing one another. Neither noticed that I'd approached.

"Nothing?" Bob was saying.

"No, no connection at all." The man pulled Bob forward, ran his calloused fingers over Bob's lips, nose, and the small creases at the corners of Bob's eyes. "I'm sorry, my child."

At the edge of the paved walk, I shuffled a foot in the sand, making enough sound to get Bob's attention. For the tiniest fraction of a second, Bob's face, as he turned to me, seemed strained, tightened, guilty. I wasn't sure I recognized him, wasn't sure that the man sitting before me was actually Bob. But then he rose, thanked the face-reader, and took my arm. We continued down the walk.

"Well?" I said.

"What?"

"What'd he say?"

Bob shook his head uncertainly.

"Nothing about your past or future?"

"Nothing much," Bob said. "He said I think too much."

"You? Really?"

"That's what he said. And that I was a Buddhist novitiate in a previous life."

"Really? You?"

"But that I was killed before becoming a real monk. In Tibet. By a tiger."

"Oh," I said. "Sorry."

Bob shrugged his shoulders. "No biggie."

We stopped to watch a fire-eater, then moved on.

"Nothing about me?" I said, finally. I'd been waiting for Bob to bring it up on his own, how we'd been together for lifetimes, how we were only fulfilling our destiny by loving one another in this life. "Anything? Hmm? Anything about me?"

"Nope," he said. "Nope. Not a word."

On the following Tuesday, during the first minute of my office hours, Trey Rothman walks in.

"I've done it," he says. "I figured it out. Finally!"

"What's that?"

"The zero proof. And it was so simple! Like you said, I was on the right path all along."

He closes the door behind him as he comes in. He sits in a chair beside my desk, perches on the front-most edge of the seat. He's leaning forward, legs primly aligned, fingertips flexing against the hollow metal spine of the spiral notebook on his lap. I can see the tiny brown hairs on his knuckles as his fingers move, the big white moons beneath the ragged nails. I look at the bones of his wrists, the tendons taut as harp strings, the veins, pulsing. I feel myself becoming aroused by every stupid, negligible detail of his body. I turn to my desk, scratch a pencil against the student paper I've been grading, pretend to make corrective marks.

"It was all because of you," Trey says.

I realize it's just flattery, just words of seduction, but for a moment I let myself be caught anyway. I sit back in my chair, clasp my hands behind my head. I imagine us in some columned outdoor chamber, far in the past. I, Socrates; he, ephebe. A young Plato, possibly. We're wearing togas trimmed in gilt. Lounging affectedly. Talking deeply, intensely, about the very structure of the world. Forms, he's saying. Ideals. The true nature of love, the duality of every living thing. And soon I realize he's surpassed me in inventiveness, that I've been outmoded by the future, by more incisive arrangements of water, earth, fire, and air, and I know for a fact that someday even he, Plato, will betray me, misquote me, put words in my mouth that I never said, attribute to me thoughts I never conceived. I won't be remembered as I truly was. I'm lost. I'm doomed.

Even my fantasies end in despair. The word escapes me before I know I've said it: "Hemlock."

"Professor?"

"Get out."

Bedtime. Naked again. We're saying nothing, Bob and I. He reaches to flip the lamp's switch, to plunge us into darkness, but I grab his arm, stop him.

Am I good for you, Bob? I say it without saying it.

I touch his chin, pull it toward me. I look into his eyes, something I rarely do. We know each other too well to look at one another so intently. Bob looks back at me, but I can't see his eyes, not really. The shadows are too strong, the lamp placed improperly.

I mount Bob's belly, feeling him breathe beneath me. I straddle him, awkwardly arranging my legs for comfort, and pull the tabletop lamp closer to us, lighting both our faces. I lean over him, look closer.

Am I in there, Bob?

Deep black mirrors stare out, surrounded by clear yellow irises. The yellowness is Bob, all that he ever was, all that he ever will be. But the tiny black centers, the blackened hearts of the daisies, the emptiness contained with them—

"What?" Bob says.

"Nothing."

THE CANALS OF MARS

Victor J. Banis

Beauty may be in the eye of the beholder, but ugly is there for everyone to see. I can afford to speak so flippantly on the subject, since I was, and I say it in all modesty, beautiful indeed.

The operative word, of course, is *was*. Was, before a vial exploded in the lab, and turned that beautiful face into a road map of Mars. In the novels, in the movies, this is where the handsome plastic surgeon rushes to the rescue, and by the next chapter-reel, I am Joan Crawford all over again, and on my way to becoming Mrs. Surgeon. Or, in my gay instance, Mister and Mister Surgeon.

Cut. First off, he was older than the hills and singularly unattractive. And he was already married and blatantly heterosexual. Don't get me wrong: I have no objections to heterosexuals, so long as they aren't too obvious. And, hell, if he had been able to make me lovely again, I'd have murdered her, had the change, and gone after the old codger regardless.

Three operations later, however, the mirror still showed me the surface of Mars. The craters had shrunk somewhat, and the canals had shifted, but it was still Mars. I balked at going under the knife a fourth time.

"No, it won't be a dramatic improvement," he said when I questioned him.

"In other words, I'm still going to look like something brought back up half eaten," I asked, and the tone in which he assured me that I would look better told me that "better" still was not going to be very good.

Which was where we left it. Notwithstanding the pleasure of lying abed in a hospital—there is nothing quite like the personal touch of your own bedpan, is there?—and all that delicious food, I promised I would get back to him, without specifying in which life.

When you are damaged, as I was, they give you lots of money, as if that would compensate for what I had lost. I was grateful, though, that I did not have to work. Not because I am all that fond of lying about vegetating, but because I did not have to face all those slipping-away eyes that I was sure to encounter.

There were not many places one could go, however, without the same problem. Jason threw in the towel and was gone. Jason who loved "the soul of me," who loved me "through and through," was through. I told myself good riddance. He was too shallow to be of much use as a lover, and I tried not to think that I had mostly been just about as shallow most of my life. I definitely tried not to remember that I loved the bastard.

I am fortunate that I am comfortable with my own company, as many are not, and there is a certain bitter comfort in wallowing in self-pity. That wears thin, though, after a while, and the walls of my little apartment seemed to shrink inward with each passing day. So, when Douglas called me, to say he was going to spend a month or two at his cottage on the shore, and would I like to come along, I jumped at the chance. I might not have in the past. I had always understood that Douglas was in love with me—whatever that meant. Jason had been in love with me, too, he said, and what had that amounted to? Who knew what "love" was? I didn't.

In the past, I might have wondered at Douglas's intentions, getting me all alone in that little cottage of his. He was Jason's friend. I liked him well enough on the few occasions when I had met him, and he was a lovely person—just not my type. Not as old as that surgeon, probably, but, really, too old for my tastes, sixty if he was a day, maybe more. I didn't really know. Anyway, what difference does a number make? There comes a point—doesn't there?—when you're just old. Though I have to admit, if you weren't hung up on age, he was a youthful-looking sixty-whatever.

They say it's an ill wind, however. With the face I now had, I did not have to worry about whether it was only my beauty that men were after.

I will give him credit. He was one of the few, the first, maybe, since the accident, who did not flinch when he saw me. He even managed to look me straight in the face, and not quickly avert his eyes.

"Pretty awful, isn't it?" I said. He had come out to help me bring my bags in.

He smiled. "I've seen worse," he said. "I used to work in a burn center."

"I hope that wasn't meant to make me feel all warm and fuzzy inside," I said, following him up the wide, shallow steps to the front door.

"No, I've got martinis waiting. That's their job."

They failed, however. All they did was lower the barriers I

had so carefully raised. The martinis, and Douglas. He was an elegant man, suave and distinguished. He was also thoughtful and gentle; I hadn't known that about him before. Of course, I had never been alone at his beach cottage with him. Never, really, been alone with him at all.

He talked of all sorts of things, movies and people we both knew and recipes and the shore and the weather and, when I could bear it no longer and the tears began to stream down my cheeks, he stopped talking and just held me. He didn't try to tell me it would be okay. He didn't try to tell me that I was still beautiful. He did not swear it would all get better, or somehow magically go away, or any of the stupid, insensitive things that others had said that had only made me feel worse. He didn't even chide me when I blubbered about the canals of Mars.

He just held me and gently kissed my cheek; not even the good one. He kissed the one that was scarred, kissed Mars's canals as if they were the most natural things on this planet. He was the first person since the accident with the courage to put his lips to my flesh; the first, even, to put his arms around me. Jason had tried, and had paled and turned away before his lips touched me, and said with a sob, as if it were his heart breaking, "I can't, I just can't." Then he left.

Douglas only held me and kissed my cheek, and when the tears stopped at last, he took me upstairs and tucked me into my bed like a little child, and brought me a cup of hot chocolate, and made me drink it, and sat and held my hand until I fell asleep.

"How long are you here for?" I asked him the next day. We were sitting on the little terrace. It was early in the season, the air still cool, but the sun warm, the ocean close enough for us to smell the brine and the seaweed. Too early for the tourists; too early, if only just, for the summer crowd.

"Till you're better," he said.

"Douglas, really, I'm all right," I said. He gave me a mocking smile. "I will be, anyway. All right, I mean. You don't have to look after me."

"I don't have to do anything," he said with a snort. He got up from his chaise lounge and offered me a hand. "Let's go for a dip, why don't we?"

"I'm sure the water's icy," I said.

"No doubt." He gave me a look that said he knew perfectly well that was not my reason for declining. "There's nobody else around," he said. "If anybody comes, we'll see them miles off."

Well, say I'm a freak if you will, but don't call me a coward. I got up without a word and set my drink aside, and started for the beach. He fell into step beside me, whistling tunelessly.

I had planned to maintain my long-suffering attitude, to punish him—for what, I wasn't quite clear, but surely no good deed should go unpunished. The water, however, wasn't nearly so cold as I had expected, and the sun got warmer as it rose in the sky, and a warm breeze ruffled my hair. The gulls jeered at me and when Douglas got tired of my standing stiffly in knee deep water, toes firmly planted in the squish of sand, he splashed me, and I yelped and kicked water in his face and before I knew it, we were horsing around like a pair of kids, laughing and ducking one another, and I actually forgot that he was an old fart and I was a horror to gaze upon.

Until he said, "Shit," loudly, and I followed his gaze, and saw a couple clambering over the rocks, heading in our direction.

I ran out of the water, grabbed my towel and started back toward the cottage, not wanting to be seen, knowing what would happen to their faces when they got close enough to see mine; and Douglas made a point of switching sides with me, so that he was between the scarred side of my face and the approaching strangers. They were probably not close enough to see, but I was grateful anyway. The canals were mine alone.

Well, of course Douglas was stuck with them too, but he seemed not to mind them. He did not pretend not to see them; he just didn't seem to mind.

Except for that intrusion, though, we were alone. His little section of rocky beach sat in a cove, so it was mostly private even as the season got on and other cottages up and down the shore were occupied. That couple, they must have been day-trippers, were the only persons we saw the whole time we were there. The only ones I saw, at any rate; he went into town every couple of days for supplies, walking the five miles or so in and out, and came back to update me: "The Jeffersons are here, they're the second cottage down," or "The Wilsons are early this year." No one came by, though. I had been here for a weekend once before, with Jason. There had been lots of neighbors dropping in, and we had made the rounds as well. Maybe he warned them off.

We swam nearly every day. I used to swim a lot, and loved it, but I was out of practice and out of shape. It was good exercise, and a good way to work off my frustrations and my anger. I swam sometimes for two hours with only the occasional pause for rest. He didn't swim that long, of course. He was old. When he began to tire and grow short of breath, he would go sit on the beach.

"And enjoy the view," he said. He looked my still handsome body up and down and gave me a wolfish leer. What he really did, of course, was stand guard, in case anyone should approach. I stopped watching for them myself and trusted him. But they didn't come.

Evenings, he fixed us martinis, and I got into the habit of preparing dinner. I had cooked in the past, but I had gotten away from it. I found now that I enjoyed it. I took unexpected pleasure in fixing the things he liked, the way he liked them. Nothing too fancy: steaks or lobster or burgers on the grill, and when it turned out we both loved it, the tuna casserole that Jason had always turned his nose up at. The one with potato chips. I caught Douglas licking the salt off the chips and smacked his hand with the spatula. Later, though, I tried it myself when he wasn't looking, and he caught me at it and smacked my hand.

"I was in the hospital for eight weeks," I told him petulantly. "You're not supposed to hit someone when they're recovering from surgery."

"Bullshit," he said, and offered me a chip to lick. He wasn't always elegant.

We ate sometimes on the terrace when it was warm enough, and at the kitchen table when it wasn't, and some evenings it was cool enough for a fire in the fireplace and we ate in front of it. There was no television, but he had a radio and a stereo, and somehow he had managed to stock a shelf with most of my favorite music. Sometimes he sat beside me, and he would shyly put his arm around me, and I would lean against him and put my head on his shoulder while we listened to music together, and watched the fire. We didn't talk much, but the silence was comfortable. Always, when he said goodnight, he kissed my cheek. The bad one.

After a week, when he started to turn away from me at my bedroom door, I said, "You don't have to go to your own room."

It took him a moment to realize what I meant. "Are you sure?" he said, uncertain and hopeful all at the same time.

"I'm sure."

I would have turned the lights out, but he wouldn't have it. "Do you have any idea how long I've dreamed of seeing you like this?" he asked. "I never thought I'd be so lucky."

I was naked by this time. He looked me up and down with undisguised pleasure while he undressed. That part of me, at least, was still fine. I was glad, for his sake as well as my own. He deserved beauty. I turned the bad cheek away.

He was naked too now, seemingly unembarrassed by his old man's body. He dropped onto the bed beside me. He looked better dressed than undressed. Old men do, don't they? I tried not to notice the spare tire, or the way his chest looked caved in, or the droop of his buns. That was just who he was. It couldn't be helped.

"That was when I was beautiful," I said. "And please don't say, 'you still are.' "

"You still are," he said.

Without thinking, I put a hand to my face. "The canals of Mars?" I said.

"Where I shall swim in ecstasy," he said and kissed the scars. I watched and listened and felt carefully with all my senses for some hint of reluctance, of disgust or even discomfort, but if he felt any, he disguised it completely.

He took hold of my hand and rubbed it across the pouch of his belly, where he had thickened about the waist. "If you'll overlook this," he said, and leaned over to kiss my lips.

It was good sex. Not great, but good. Of course, sex had been a solitary pastime for me since the accident. Jack off and think of Jason, think of Jason and jack off. Maybe at this point in time, anybody would have made it seem good. I don't know. I don't think so. I suppose that is one of the advantages of age, though: practice makes you, if not perfect, pretty adept. He was. He made love to me. I had never experienced that before. Lots of sex, none hotter than with Jason, but no one had ever made love to me. It was nice. I kissed him when it was over, and kissing him, actually forgot about how I looked. He stayed the night in my bed. I slept comfortably in the crook of his arm. I realized when I woke in the morning that I had forgotten, too, how old he was.

After that, we slept together every night. He could not have been more tender, more loving, and I stirred myself to be as good as I could be for him as well. It got better, our sex. I wanted it to, and it did, it got very much better. I stopped jacking off remembering Jason. I didn't stop remembering Jason, but I stopped jacking off remembering him. Stopped jacking off altogether, to tell the truth. Who had anything left to shoot, the way we were going at it? He was insatiable. The old goat. It was flattering. Exhausting, but flattering.

One night when we finished, he rolled on his back with a gasp and said, "If you keep it up like that, you're going to kill me. I'm an old man, remember?"

"You're not so old," I said. And, to my surprise, I meant it. I'd been to bed with men forty years his junior who weren't the lover he was. Or, maybe they were. What I really mean is that I hadn't gotten the pleasure, the same kind of pleasure, from them that I did from him. Maybe that was in part the pleasure that I was giving. I had never thought of it like that before: taking pleasure in giving it. I wanted to make him happy. I wanted to please him. When I did, and he made it quite obvious that I did, it made me happy too.

That was a new one for me.

We divided up the housecleaning. The one who scrubbed the bathroom got to pick the music. Since that was not one of my favorite chores, we listened to a lot of Sarah Vaughn and Dinah Washington, both new to me, but I quickly fell in love. It would no doubt have looked a little funny to someone else, him scrubbing the tub and me mopping the kitchen, and both of us bellowing "All of Me," along with Dinah. His lack of pitch didn't seem all that important. It was a while before I realized: I hadn't sung in years. Even before the scars. Where, I wondered, had the music gone?

I learned that he liked to read aloud. I'd never had anyone do that for me, but I found that I enjoyed that too. He had a lovely reading voice, multicolored and far more musical than his singing voice. He read *Vanity Fair*, a chapter an evening. Listening to him, watching the fire, it was easy to sink into the story. Becky Sharp winked at me from the flames. I liked her.

I liked the beach at night, too, maybe because I didn't have to think about anybody seeing me. Anybody but Douglas. I would sit and watch the surf, and he would lie on his back and gaze up at the stars.

"I wonder," he said one night, "when we look at them, is it the stars twinkling, or our eyes?"

"My eyes don't twinkle," I told him.

"Oh, but they do," he said, sitting up with a grin and looking into them. "They get like Christmas lights when you're about to come."

"That is so ridiculous," I said. "You are so full of shit."

We made love in the warm sand, the murmur of the waves like muted strings to our dissonant chorus of sighs and moans. He went down on me, and just as I was about to go off, he jumped up over me and said, "There, they're sparkling like crazy."

I couldn't help laughing, and he laughed with me, and hugged me. I had almost forgotten how to laugh.

After a while, I lifted my head and looked down at myself. "Were you planning on finishing that?" I asked.

"Try to stop me," he said, sliding down in the sand.

Sometimes, after swimming, his hips bothered him. "A touch of arthritis," he said and I quickly got into the habit of massaging them for him.

"Are you going to massage me all over?" he asked with a naughty grin when I told him to strip and lie down on the floor.

"I'm going to work on the parts that are sore."

"Oh, have I got an ache here," he said with a laugh, and cupped his balls in his hand. I slapped his butt hard.

"Now you've got one there, too," I said. But I kept my word and massaged that for him as well. Everywhere he said he ached.

He kept finding new places.

He was getting ready to walk into town one day—it was a month or more after I had arrived there, though the time had passed with astonishing rapidity—when he asked with a sly expression if I wanted to go along.

"Don't be fucking stupid," I snapped, angry out of all proportion. "Did you plan to sell tickets?"

"Come here," he said. He took my hand and brought me into his bedroom. There was a large mirror over his dresser. Mine had none. This one and the little one on the medicine cabinet were the only ones in the cottage. I could shave in the medicine cabinet mirror without looking at the scars. The whiskers didn't grow on that side. There were advantages to having your skin burned off. Think about it, if you don't like shaving.

When I saw where he was leading me, I held back. "Don't," I said. "Don't be cruel. You know I don't want to see."

"But you do," he said, and would not let go of me, and all but dragged me to the mirror. "Look." I automatically turned the bad side away from the glass, but he put a hand on my chin and stubbornly turned my face.

It would be dramatic and exciting to say that the scars had disappeared. They hadn't; but even I could see that they had faded considerably. I still looked like the surface of Mars, but viewed through an out-of-focus telescope. Someone—not everyone, but probably one or two here or there—could look at it and not want to vomit.

I put a hand up and ran my fingers over my cheek, as if to confirm that it really was my face, my present face, and not some photograph he had taped up to fool me. I couldn't think what to say. I shook my head, bewildered.

He grinned and kissed my cheek, the bad side—the not-quite-so-bad side now—and said, "I'll be back in an hour or so. Anything you want?"

It was maybe a week after that, the day he went down to the beach alone. The weather had turned cool, and I decided to stay on the terrace and read. I read and dozed, and thought about what had happened to my face. I had only looked once since that first day, afraid that I would realize I was merely a victim of wishful thinking. It wasn't that, though. The scars were still there, but the ugly raw-liver red of the canals had faded to patches of dusty rose. I couldn't understand it. I wanted to think about it. The doctor had given me a special salve. I hadn't bothered using it, thinking there was little chance of significant improvement. Now I applied it assiduously morning and night, not minding the rotten-potato stink. If Douglas minded it, he never said.

Still, I was afraid to look, afraid to jinx whatever was happening.

Douglas shouted something from the beach, interrupting my reverie. I sat up and looked. He was holding a starfish aloft, waving it for me like a flag. I laughed and waved back, and he tossed it into the water again. Some would have kept it for a trophy, letting the living thing within the shell die. He wouldn't. He was too good a man. I had never known a better one, my whole life, or one—it surprised me to realize this—whose company pleased me more. Our days had flown by. How could I have thought him a bore, in the past? How could I have been so vacuous?

He began to climb up the rocks, coming back. I watched him and it occurred to me all at once that he looked different. His waist was trimmer, and that little paunch had shrunk away. Seeing him like this, at the distance, he might have passed for a man in his forties. His early forties. All that swimming, I thought; all those hikes into town and back.

Or, something.

"Something is happening to us," I said.

He smiled; I don't think I had ever actually noticed what a sweet smile he had. "What do you mean?" he asked.

"Well, look at us. Look at you. You look fifteen years younger than you did when we came here. Twenty years, maybe."

He lifted his head to look down at his naked body. "I've lost some weight. That's your cooking. I lived on pizza in town."

"But it's not just your weight," I said. I rolled onto my side and ran a hand across the surface of his belly, the way I had done our first night in bed. "Look, it's hard as a rock."

"That's not the only thing, in case you hadn't noticed," he said. He took my hand and put it on his erection.

"Okay, case in point," I said, but I did not take my hand away. "We just fucked, not even ten minutes ago. When was the last time you were raring to go so soon afterward?"

"The last time? Probably I was jacking off thinking about you," he said. He rolled over to face me, and took me in his arms, and kissed me, and for a while, we had no more conversation.

Really, he was insatiable. The old goat. Damned good, now, but insatiable.

But he wasn't an old goat anymore, either. I couldn't stop thinking about it. I couldn't stop looking at him. Before, at the beginning, I had mostly averted my eyes when he was naked, embarrassed for him, turned off for myself.

It wasn't just curiosity that had me staring at him whenever I could now, though I was fascinated by the changes in him; it almost seemed as if I could see them happening. I looked because he was terrific to look at. It wasn't only his body. He might have had the world's most successful face-lift. The jowls were gone, the laugh lines, the furrows on his brow. His thin hair was thicker, and lustrous. He had always been handsome in an old-man way, handsome-distinguished. Now, he was just plain hot. Had he always been? Had I always been blind?

"Is this still sore?" I asked him, massaging one hip.

"Not since you started working on it," he said. "You've got magic in your hands."

I stared at him. At his round, hard butt. I still would not look at my scarred face. I was too afraid of what I would see. Or not see. But his butt was lovely to look at. I looked every chance I got. Both of us enjoyed the massages.

Of course, he wasn't going to let me avoid that other sight.

"Look," he said, holding the mirror up in front of me.

I turned away from it, like a vampire afraid that he will see no reflection. "No, I don't want to," I said sharply. "I'm afraid."

"Look," he said insistently and again put the mirror in front of my face. I had no choice but to look into it.

"What do you see?" he asked.

"I see…" I hesitated. Did I really see what I thought I saw? It was almost—not quite, but very close, to what I had used to see, in the past; before the accident. My face. Not that hideous thing that had been foisted on me, but the beautifully sculpted cheekbones, the mouth that Jason had always called "too kissable," the little rounded chin.

The smooth, porcelain skin. "It's me," I said, in wonder. "The canals. They're gone." Nearly, at any rate. I had to lean toward the glass, peer closely, to see their faint vestiges.

"Yes. I wanted to say something sooner, but I wanted to be sure," he said.

"I'm beautiful," I said. I put my hand up to touch my face, still not able to comprehend.

"You always have been," he said. "To me. It's just the surface stuff that's changing. That's really not all that important. There never really were any canals, you know." I looked my puzzlement at him. "On Mars, I mean," he said. "It was a bum lens in somebody's telescope, badly focused, the way I understand it, and somebody mistranslated the word *channels,* so it was all a misunderstanding. Later, when they could see it better, could look at it through a proper lens, and somebody corrected the translation, they realized there weren't any canals. Never had been."

"But mine were. And now they're gone." I looked at him, kneeling over the bed, at his firm, youthful body. "We've both changed. You look entirely different as well. What can it mean?"

"Maybe," he said, putting the mirror aside, "We were just looking through the wrong lens. Maybe we're just seeing one another now through the eyes of love. Maybe we had the word wrong, too. Maybe what we thought that was, was something else."

Love. I thought about that for a while. Was that what this was? It wasn't like anything I had felt before, nothing like what I had thought love was. Nothing, for instance, compared to what I had felt in the past, for Jason. And yet, it felt good, in a way I had never felt for anyone before. It felt good knowing he loved me. Whatever it was I felt for him, that felt good too. I was afraid to call it love, though. What I had called love in the past had gone from me in a twinkling, had drowned in those canals on Mars. Before they got the telescope straightened out.

He saw my expression. "What?" he asked.

"I was just thinking."

"About?"

I looked directly at him. "About Jason," I said.

I could see that it had hurt him. His eyes, so bright a moment before, went dull, although he managed to keep a faint smile on his lips. "Still hurt, does it?"

I sighed. I couldn't lie to him. Maybe that was love, when you can't lie to someone. How would I know? About love? "Yes."

"You're thinking, if he saw you now, just like you used to be, that he would fall in love with you all over again."

Was that what I wanted? I wasn't sure. I couldn't say the idea wasn't tempting. I remembered the last time, the regret and the shame on Jason's face. What would it be worth, to see his expression change to something else? What was I willing to pay for that satisfaction? I said nothing, and after a moment, he read my silence, and sighed also.

"Well, there's only one way to know, isn't there?" he said. He sat up, and reached for his clothes where he had tossed them on the floor when we had undressed so hurriedly. I looked at his back, so firm, the muscles rippling the way a young man's muscles did, his cheeks, when he raised them to slip his boxers on, round and firm and pale, as if they were carved of alabaster. I thought of how sleek they felt when I ran my hand over them, massaging him. I almost reached out to touch him.

Almost.

We drove into the city that same day, hardly talking. We left my car at the beach. "I can bring it in for you later," he said. He never stopped thinking of ways to make things easier for me. Even now. Even taking me back to Jason.

He stopped at the curb in front of my apartment. I sat, looking for a moment up at the window on the third floor. Jason had promised to look after things, but I could see that the geranium in the window was dead.

I glanced sideways at Douglas. He was trying to smile, but the droop of his jowls and the furrows on his brow turned his smile sad. In the afternoon light, the pouches under his eyes looked like wet teabags.

"It's all right," he said, and put his hand atop mine. "Really, I mean it. You can't know how happy you've made me these last couple of months. Whatever you decide now, it won't take anything away from that. It won't make me love you any less."

I looked down at his old man's hand, knobby and wrinkled. I started to reach for the mirror over the visor, and changed my mind. I didn't need to look. I didn't need to see Jason, either. I already knew what he was. And wasn't.

"Take me home," I said.

"Home?" He glanced past me, at the apartment building, wanting to be certain, not daring to misunderstand.

"The cottage. Our cottage. Please."

He was silent for a moment. "You're sure?" he asked.

"Yes," I said. I had never in my life been more sure of anything.

He looked at me long and hard. I looked back, full face, not turning my cheek away as I had gotten into the habit of doing. I didn't need to now. I knew that.

Finally, he leaned across the seat and touched my cheek, the scarred one, with his lips, and I turned my face and found his lips with mine, and kissed him.

He put the car in gear, and drove away from the curb. About halfway to the cottage, he began to sing, "All of Me."

"You know, you never do get on pitch," I said with some asperity.

"Well, then, you sing it," he said.

I did. We sang it together at the tops of our lungs. People in the cars we passed stared. Some of them smiled. Some of them saw into the car, and looked away. Douglas grinned sideways at me, a boyish, devilish grin, and took my hand and put it on his lap.

"Guess what I want to do when we get home," he said.

"You old goat," I said, but I did not take my hand away.

ABOUT THE AUTHORS

VICTOR J. BANIS, lecturer, former writing instructor, and early rabble-rouser for gay rights and freedom of the press, is author ("...the master's touch in storytelling..."—*Publishers Weekly*) of more than one hundred and fifty books, including the novel *Longhorns* (Carroll & Graf, 2007). Borgos/Wildside Press is reprinting more than twenty of his out-of-print novels, as well as five new books. His verse and shorter pieces have appeared in numerous journals (Blithe House Quarterly) and anthologies including *Charmed Lives* and *Paws and Reflect*. A native of Ohio, and a longtime Californian, he lives and writes now in West Virginia's beautiful Blue Ridge.

DALE CHASE has been happily writing male erotica for nearly a decade, with more than one hundred stories published in various magazines and anthologies. Her first literary effort appeared in the *Harrington Gay Men's Fiction Quarterly*. She has completed a collection of Victorian gentlemen's erotica, *The*

Company He Keeps. Chase lives near San Francisco and is working on a collection of ghostly male erotica.

KAL COBALT is a native Oregonian who recently relocated to Portland. Read more of Kal's work in *Country Boys, Hot Gay Erotica*, Velvet Mafia (www.velvetmafia.com), *Distant Horizons*, edited by Greg Herren, and *Best Fantastic Erotica*, edited by Cecilia Tan. Find out more at www.kalcobalt.com.

JAMESON CURRIER is the author of a novel, *Where the Rainbow Ends*, and two collections of short stories, most recently *Desire, Lust, Passion, Sex*.

JACK FRITSCHER, celebrating his fiftieth year as a published author, hosts the free gay research site www.jackfritscher.com. He is author of *Some Dance to Remember: A Memoir-Novel of San Francisco 1970-1982* and *Gay San Francisco: Eyewitness Drummer: A Narrative History of the Sex, Art, Politics, and Salon around* Drummer Magazine. Email welcome: jack@jackfritscher.com

SHANNA GERMAIN writes in a number of genres, but erotica is her favorite. Her poems, essays, and short stories have appeared in places like *Absinthe Literary Review, Best American Erotica 2007, Best Bondage Erotica, Cowboy Lover, He's on Top,* and Salon. She loves to hear from readers; visit her online at www.shannagermain.com.

T. HITMAN is the nom-de-porn of a full-time professional writer who routinely contributes to a number of national magazines and fiction anthologies, and who once worked as a screenwriter for a classic Paramount science fiction series. He's been writing more romantic fiction since early 2005, after moving into his small cottage in the big woods with his longtime partner and their rescue cat, as evidenced by his autobiographical story, "The Bike Path."

SHAUN LEVIN's collection of short stories, *A Year of Two Summers*, was published in 2005. A novella, *Seven Sweet Things*, was published in 2003. His stories appear in anthologies as diverse as *Between Men*, *Modern South African Stories*, *Boyfriends from Hell*, *Best Gay Erotica 2000*, *2002*, and *2004*, and *The Slow Mirror: New Fiction by Jewish Writers*. He is the editor of *Chroma: A Queer Literary Journal*. See more at shaunlevin.com and chromajournal.co.uk.

MATTHEW LOWE is a young Australian writer. His work has appeared in the *Griffith Review,* Australia's leading literary journal. In 2006, he received an Express Media Mentorship Award, allowing him to work alongside prominent gay author and poet Andy Quan.

MAX PIERCE's debut novel is the gothic mystery *The Master of Seacliff*. When not waxing romantic, Max can be found dividing his time between fiction and journalism, and his musings on gay culture and Hollywood history have appeared online for *The Advocate* and other national publications. He previously contributed to the vampire anthology *Blood Lust*. He lives in Los Angeles. More at www.maxpierce.com.

ROB ROSEN lives in San Francisco with his handsome partner, Kenny. He is the author of *Sparkle: The Queerest Book You'll Ever Love* and the forthcoming *Divas Las Vegas*. His short stories have appeared in numerous journals, magazines, websites, and anthologies, most notably: *Mentsh: On Being Jewish and Queer; I Do/I Don't: Queers on Marriage; Best Gay Love Stories 2006; Best Gay Romance; Best Gay Love Stories: New York City; Truckers,* and *The Queer Collection: Poetry and Prose 2007.* Please visit him at his website, www.therobrosen.com, or email him at robrosen@therobrosen.com.

SIMON SHEPPARD is the editor of *Homosex: Sixty Years of Gay Erotica,* and the author of *In Deep: Erotic Stories; Kinkorama: Dispatches From the Front Lines of Perversion; Sex Parties 101,* and the award-winning *Hotter Than Hell and Other Stories.* His work has appeared in about two hundred and fifty anthologies, including many editions of *The Best American Erotica* and many, many of *Best Gay Erotica.* He writes the syndicated column "Sex Talk," the online serial "Dirty Boys Club," and hangs out romantically at www.simonsheppard.com.

JASON SHULTS's work has appeared online in Blithe House Quarterly and Velvet Mafia, and in several print publications, including the anthology *Fresh Men: New Voices in Gay Fiction.* He owns a bookstore in Tucson, Arizona, and is currently at work on a novel.

J. M. SNYDER writes gay erotic/romantic fiction. Originally self-published, Snyder now works with the e-publishers Amber Heat Press and Aspen Mountain Press. Snyder's highly erotic short gay fiction has been published online at Ruthie's Club, Tit-Elation, and Amazon Shorts, as well as in anthologies published by Cleis Press, Haworth Press, and Alyson Books. A full bibliography, as well as free stories, excerpts, purchasing info, and contests, can be found on the author's website at http://jmsnyder.net.

NATTY SOLTESZ, under the pseudonym "bacteriaburger," has published fiction on the *Nifty Erotic Stories Archive* since 2001. Recently he's contributed to the magazines *Men*, *Mandate*, and *Handjobs*, the websites Clean Sheets and Velvet Mafia and *Ultimate Gay Erotica 2008*. He's now working with director Joe Gage on a script for an upcoming porn movie. He lives in Pittsburgh with his lover. Check out his website, www. bacteriaburger.com.

JAY STARRE, residing on English Bay in Vancouver, Canada, writes fiction for gay men's magazines, including *Men* and *Torso*, and has also contributed to more than forty anthologies, including *Travelrotica*, *Manhandled*, *Bear Lust,* and *Bad Boys.*

ABOUT THE EDITOR

RICHARD LABONTÉ has edited the *Best Gay Erotica* series since 1997. He writes the occasional newsletter, *Books To Watch Out For*, and the fortnightly book review column, "Book Marks," distributed by Q Syndicate. With Lawrence Schimel, he is co-editor of *The Future is Queer* and *First Person Queer*, for Arsenal Pulp Press. He has edited *Hot Gay Erotica*, *Country Boys*, *Best Gay Bondage*, *Boys in Heat*, and *Where the Boys Are* for Cleis Press, where he is also an editor at large. He lives on Bowen Island, British Columbia, sixty seconds from the Pacific Ocean, and on a farm in rural eastern Ontario, surrounded by two hundred acres of hay fields.